A WITCH'S WORK

is never done

Kate Moseman

A Witch's Work is Never Done

Copyright © 2020 by Kate Moseman

This is a work of fiction. Names, characters, places, and incidents either are the product of the author's imagination or are used fictitiously. Any resemblance to actual persons, living or dead, events, or locales is entirely coincidental.

First Edition

ISBN 978-1-7345144-2-1 (ebook)
ISBN 978-1-7345144-3-8 (paperback)

Published by:
Fortunella Press

À Mon Seul Désir

PART I

RAYA

1

If witches really could fly on brooms, it would have saved a fortune in airfare.

Raya pulled herself out of the cramped seat the moment the plane shuddered to a halt on the tarmac. She stepped sideways into the aisle of the plane only to be knocked back into her seat in an ungainly sprawl.

The culprit didn't even bother to murmur a perfunctory *"Pardon, madame."*

Or would it be *"Pardon, mademoiselle"*?

Was she still considered a mademoiselle?

Raya shook her head and pulled herself up all over again. This time, she hip checked the offending passenger and took a place beneath the overhead bin. She seized the handle of her carry-on and hauled.

Too hard.

Her carry-on tumbled free, striking the seat below and bouncing off, knocking Raya full in the chest and sending her backward. She felt the impact as she hit the person behind her.

Of course, she'd knocked someone sprawling into their own seat.

It figured.

Raya turned to apologize. "I'm sorry, ma'am—"

Her victim let loose a torrent of French containing the words "*stupide*" and "*Americaine*."

Raya didn't need a French phrase book to translate that. She made soothing, apologetic noises as she settled her bag on her shoulder, then quick-marched down the aisle as fast as she could.

Discretion, after all, was the better part of valor.

Raya stumbled only a little as she picked up speed going down the ramp to the airport terminal. She emerged into a crowd of people, and, having no better plans, followed the flow past a large bank of windows looking out toward an adjacent building decorated with red, white, and blue neon.

A lock of hair broke loose from her bun. She pressed her free hand to the back of her head, ensuring that her beloved wand remained firmly in place tucked inside the thick twist of hair.

The innocuous stick of wood, topped with a rather undistinguished crystal, rode jauntily in its accustomed place.

Raya sighed and sped up again, approaching what appeared to be an endless moving walkway that angled down a corridor. She'd have to find something to eat, and soon. The leftover in-flight cookies she'd stuffed in her pockets weren't going to cut it. She ripped open a packet anyway and tipped the crumby contents into her mouth as she continued down the walkway, managing to spill less than half of it down her front.

France was getting off to a great start.

She knocked off some of the crumbs and kept moving, glancing up at the oncoming signage, which was blessedly written in French and English. The signs led her to a second walkway, this one encased in clear plexiglass, allowing a view of the bustling, multi-level terminal with similar walkways stretching in all directions, punctuated by gleaming banks of windows.

At the baggage carousel, Raya peered hopefully at each oncoming suitcase.

Hope dwindled as the carousel emptied.

She had no choice but to seek out the airline's customer service booth.

Raya dug around in her carry-on and pulled the pocket French phrasebook to the surface. Gripping it over her heart like a crucifix for warding off vampires, she approached the counter.

An impossibly chic woman stood behind the desk. "Bonjour, madame," she said.

Raya remembered the baggage claim sign over the walkway. "Uh, yes, bonjour. My…*bagage*—"

"*Mon bagage*," the woman corrected.

Raya blinked at her. Did she really think right now was the time for a language lesson? "Sure. *Mon bagage*." She flipped the phrasebook open and prepared to further murder the French language. "*J'ai perdu mon bagage*," she finished triumphantly.

The airline representative looked her up and down.

Raya could only imagine what went through her mind as she took in the view of Raya's disheveled hair, fading makeup, and a black t-shirt that read "Don't Make Me Drop a House on You."

The woman sighed and switched to English. "Please give me your address. We will send it to your hotel."

"Couldn't you check for it? Maybe it's still here," said Raya.

"We will send it to your hotel."

Clearly the woman did not wish to be bothered by rumpled Americans with petty luggage problems.

Raya removed the wand from her bun. The bun poofed open, sending her hair tumbling down. She inhaled slowly, cradling the wand in her hand, and exhaled gently, imagining her breath casting a web like spider's silk across the counter. A spell wasn't a bomb. A spell was a butterfly wing flapped in the right place, at the right time. "Please?"

The woman's expression softened ever so slightly. She regarded Raya with something closer to pity than contempt. "Very well. Wait here."

Fifteen minutes and one formerly missing suitcase later, Raya took off at a jog to catch the next train into Paris. She took one escalator after another, continuing downward from level to level, until she reached the train platform a little out of breath but smiling to herself.

She boarded the train with her bags and found a seat, letting her gaze drift over her fellow passengers.

Were there any other witches aboard?

Witches were rare, to be sure, but there would be an unusual concentration of practitioners converging on Paris today to attend the international witchcraft convention.

Raya looked for tell-tale signs: a crystal, perhaps, or unusual tattoos. Even a scent could be a giveaway.

No witches. No demons, either, that she could see. Demons stood out like they were highlighted in red, and tended to avoid witches like cats avoid water. Raya had encountered precious few of the lords of Hell.

When you conjured a demon, you never knew what you were going to get.

Raya watched the lights of the Paris suburbs flash by outside the window until her grumbling stomach reminded her of her hunger. She turned from the window to rummage hopefully in the bottom of her bag.

A tapping noise interrupted her digging.

Raya looked up. She glanced around the train car, but saw nothing unusual. She returned her attention to the search and reached deep into the bag, spurred on by the faint crinkling of a wrapper.

The tapping sound, now more insistent, sounded even closer.

Her hand seized something at the very bottom. Was the tapping coming from outside? She glanced out the window as she carefully tugged the crinkly item up.

Raya stifled a scream as a shadowed floating head appeared outside the window. She recoiled in panic and knocked the bag over, sending its contents across the floor.

The head outside the window floated closer, revealing a finely shaped nose and an insolent grin.

As Raya's eyes adjusted, she perceived the floating head's shock of thick hair, insouciant in its effortlessly tousled style—and ruffling attractively in the wind coming off the speeding train.

"Phoenix, you bastard!"

Phoenix laughed heartily at her expostulation, the sound of it muted by the glass between them, but his expression was perfectly clear. He flapped his deep red wings with supreme unconcern.

Of course it had been utter folly to allow a demon to follow her to Paris—no matter how good-looking he was or how he occasionally managed to make her laugh.

No, not folly. Sheer madness.

Only then did she realize how she must look to the passengers sharing the train car. She snuck a furtive look around.

The other passengers quickly looked away.

Obviously, she'd made herself out to be a crazy person who shouted at windows and dumped her belongings on the floor.

Raya shot a venomous look at the winged figure outside the window before sheepishly collecting the contents of her bag from the floor.

The crinkly wrapper turned out to be just that: an empty wrapper.

Raya heaved a sigh that turned into a frustrated growl. She never should have allowed Phoenix to come along on this trip, even if he promised to behave himself and stay out of her way.

She'd flown by herself, since demons—damn them and their wings—didn't need to fly coach. Phoenix was supposed to meet her in Paris, not scare the daylights out of her on a train.

Then again, demons weren't known for their good behavior.

She looked out the window to see if he was still amusing himself by making faces.

He was nowhere to be seen.

Great.

Raya settled into her seat, stewing with annoyance and hunger and pique.

When the train finally pulled into the station, she bolted up, ignoring the stares of her fellow passengers, and charged out of the train onto the platform.

Phoenix leaned against a nearby column wearing his usual all-black ensemble, this time topped with a black leather jacket, looking as normal as a demon could look. "Miss me, Witchiepoo?"

"Shut up, demon." She brandished her suitcase. "At least make yourself useful and carry this."

"Do I look like a porter?"

"You look like an ass. Carry the suitcase." Raya strode on.

Phoenix caught up. "Do you even know where you're going?" Amusement rang in his voice.

Raya stopped. She didn't have the slightest idea where to go, but Phoenix didn't need to know that. "Of course I do."

"You don't want me to show you?" Phoenix dripped condescension.

"If I had any sense, I wouldn't even be hanging out with you." Raya looked around for a hint of where to get a taxi.

They had taxis in Paris, right?

"What, afraid your witchy credibility will be ruined by socializing with demonkind?"

Raya's attention returned to Phoenix. "Don't state the obvious. You knew you would have to make yourself scarce when we got here. That was the deal. You get to come along, but you stay out of sight and—"

"Out of your way. Yes, I know." He rolled his eyes. "But you're such a delicate fawn, lost in the big woods—"

Raya punched him in the arm.

"Ow!" he said.

"Delicate, am I?"

"I take it back."

"I think I've seen enough of you for one day." Raya spotted the taxi sign and started moving.

"Would you like me to be invisible?"

"You wouldn't be invisible to me. You were invisible to the people on the train and that caused enough trouble. It's really awkward, you know—reacting to someone who isn't there. Or should I say 'isn't all there'?"

"Hilarious. Sometimes I forget how amusing you are, Raya. Until I'm stuck with you for more than five minutes."

Raya hailed a taxi like she'd done it a million times, when in fact she'd only seen it done in movies. "They say absence makes the heart grow fonder, Phoenix. Why don't you try it?"

"Or what? Are you going to banish me?"

"Don't be an idiot."

A taxi pulled up to the curb.

"That's what your witch friends would do."

Raya took the suitcase from him and handed it to the cabbie. "Don't tempt me."

"Good to know where I stand, then," said Phoenix.

Raya slid into the backseat. "See you later, Phoenix. Try to stay out of trouble."

"No promises. *Au revoir!*"

He slammed the taxi door shut before she could fire off a comeback.

2

From the back seat, Raya handed the taxi driver a slip of paper with the name and address of her hotel. "Hotel, please. You understand?"

The driver nodded and said something in French that sounded reassuring.

Raya hugged herself and bounced her knees up and down in excitement.

Paris! The dream of a lifetime finally coming true. She resisted the urge to blow kisses out the cab window to the people on the sidewalks. She settled for drinking in the sights as they sped past the Louvre and over the Seine into the 7th *arrondissement*, or district, of Paris.

What a view Phoenix would have from the air, the *arrondissements* laid out like the chambers of a nautilus, spiraling out from the center of the city.

She almost envied him. In fact, she did envy him. Not that she'd trust him to fly her around, of course. He'd probably drop her just for fun.

The driver pulled the cab over and gestured toward a nearby building. *"L'hôtel."*

"Merci." Raya gathered her things and hopped onto the sidewalk. She looked up and down the street in the darkness, searching for an open restaurant.

Not that a restaurant was even an option while lugging her bags.

She threw open the hotel door with more force than necessary and approached the front desk. Raising her index finger in the universal sign for "wait," she scribbled her name on a piece of paper and handed it to the clerk manning the desk.

Bemused, he took the paper and glanced from the writing to her face and back again. He smiled. "You are checking in?"

Raya beamed. "You speak English?"

"Of course. I speak English, French, and Arabic." He handed the paper to Raya and tapped the keys of his keyboard. "How do you like Paris so far?"

"It's beautiful."

"Much of it. And the night has its own charm, yes?"

Raya nodded, relieved beyond words to leave the phrasebook in her bag.

"Here we are." He handed a key across the desk. "And if you need anything while you are here—I am Ahmed."

"Thank you, Ahmed." Raya shouldered her bag.

He made a tut-tutting noise. *"Merci,* yes? You must learn some French while you are here."

Raya racked her brain for the right word. *"Merci beaucoup,* Ahmed."

"You are learning already!"

After dragging her luggage up the narrow flight of stairs, Raya deposited her bags in the small but clean room and returned to the ground level in search of food.

"Back already?" said Ahmed.

"Is there somewhere I can get something to eat this late?"

"Walk to the cross-street on the right and you will find a small supermarket. To the left you will find a bakery. Take your pick."

Raya thanked him and crossed the hotel threshold into the night.

A supermarket promised a solid meal, perhaps a pre-made sandwich or a ready-to-eat tray of fruit and cheese.

On the other hand…

Visions of Parisian pastries danced in Raya's head.

She turned decisively to the left.

She found the little bakery lit up from within like a glass jewel box filled with treats instead of gems. Raya nearly pressed her nose against the glass like a small child. Instead, she opened the door and stepped inside.

"Bonjour, madame," called the shopkeeper from behind the counter.

One of the very few things Raya knew about France was that you must greet the shopkeeper upon entering the shop or asking for assistance, so she summoned her best French accent—which, in all honesty, was probably terrible—and offered a greeting that made up in gusto what it lacked in polish.

The shopkeeper, a tall blonde woman dressed in the white clothing of a baker, did not offer a smile in return. Instead, she regarded Raya gravely.

Raya swallowed. Her limited French vocabulary deserted her. She pointed, tentatively, at a stack of pink macarons, then held up three fingers.

A ghost of a smile flitted across the shopkeeper's face. She added the treats to a small box and started to close it.

"No! I mean—please? A few more things?" Raya gestured for her to wait, then pointed to a tray of chocolate croissants and held up two fingers.

The shopkeeper attempted to place the two croissants into the small box, realized it was too small, and transferred everything to a larger box.

Encouraged, Raya waved the shopkeeper over and pointed to what appeared to be an array of savory mini-quiches. She held up four fingers.

The shopkeeper raised a questioning eyebrow and held up four fingers in return.

Raya rubbed her stomach. "So hungry!"

The shopkeeper shrugged eloquently and loaded the quiches into the box, filling it to the very top.

Raya spotted eclairs. "One of those?" She pointed with a hopeful expression.

This time, the shopkeeper closed the box and retrieved the eclair with a small sheet of waxed paper. She mimed taking a bite, then handed the eclair to Raya.

"For now? That's perfect. Thank you. *Merci beaucoup.*" Raya stopped herself from gobbling the pastry and instead attempted to take a dainty bite, leaving only a little bit of cream filling on her upper lip. She paid and waved goodbye with the eclair as she left.

As she walked toward the hotel, she heard the tell-tale flutter of wings behind her. "You can't startle me now, Phoenix," she called.

He emerged from the darkness to walk by her side. "What, and spill your dinner on the Paris sidewalk? Even I have some manners."

"Really? I hadn't noticed."

"Hold on." He touched her lightly on the shoulder to stop her forward movement.

"What?" She paused on the sidewalk, still chewing a bite of eclair.

"You have a mustache. Don't go walking around Paris with a mustache."

She glided her tongue over her upper lip. "Better?"

He blinked. "Good enough."

They resumed walking side by side.

"Did you follow me all the way here?" Raya licked chocolate from her finger.

"I couldn't let you get murdered on your first night in Paris."

"But the second night would be okay?" She elbowed him lightly.

"Oh, I'd make sure it didn't happen until at least a week in. Otherwise you'd miss all the best sightseeing."

"Good to know you care."

Phoenix was oddly quiet for a moment. "Do you have any plans yet?"

"Plans?"

"Yes, woman—plans. Those things sensible mortals make? Ever heard of them?"

"Who needs plans? I'm in Paris. I'm going to the world's biggest witchcraft convention. Isn't that enough?"

"Right," said Phoenix. "I mean, I don't have any plans either."

They walked in silence.

"Unless you wanted to grab something to eat sometime?"

Raya laughed. "Are you asking me to dinner?"

Phoenix glowered. "Of course not. But I thought maybe I could prevent your imminent murder by showing you around the city a bit."

"That's weirdly thoughtful of you." Raya pulled a macaron out of the box and bit into it.

"If I don't murder you first, that is."

"Likewise," said Raya. "Here, stuff this in your mouth and stop talking." She pressed a macaron to his full and somewhat pouty lips, giving him no choice but to seize it with his teeth.

While he dealt with the unexpected mouthful, she took the opportunity to steer the conversation. "I want to see something cool. I can see tourist stuff on my own time. Where's the demon dive bar?"

Phoenix snorted. "Not that you'd be welcome."

"I didn't ask for a welcome. I asked for something cool. Impress me." She tore off a hunk of chocolate croissant and popped it in her mouth.

"Yes, Your Witchiness. I live to serve." Phoenix bowed mockingly.

"Knock it off. It's not like that." Raya felt heat flare over her face.

"Not anymore, anyway."

"Who's the greater power, here, anyway? Me? With my little

wand and barely noticeable spells? Or you, with your wings and your invisibility and your dream walking and your—"

"Spectacular good looks?" Phoenix ran his hand through his hair.

Raya stopped. "Who said I didn't have spectacular good looks?"

"I didn't say that," said Phoenix.

"You implied it." Raya spotted the hotel ahead and marched on.

"I did nothing of the kind."

Raya scoffed.

"Now, hang on a minute, witch." He skidded in front of her. "You're lacking a lot of things—tact, sense, and humility, for a start—but you're not lacking in the looks department."

"'Not lacking'?"

"Fine, you ridiculous mortal, you're a good-looking witch. Is that what you want? Happy now?"

Raya made a self-satisfied noise and continued walking. "You think I'm pretty!"

Phoenix rolled his eyes. "Now I'll never hear the end of it."

"Phoenix and Raya, sitting in a tree—"

"Shut up, witch."

"K-I-S-S—"

"Did I mention you also never know when to stop?"

"Then we have that in common as well," said Raya. She made smooching sounds in his direction, then stopped when she realized they'd already reached the hotel. "This is where I leave you. Try not to pine."

Their gazes locked.

Phoenix leaned toward her. "Try not to get murdered."

3

The dawn of the next day delivered an avalanche of jet lag. Raya headed out in search of coffee.

Paris sparkled in the morning light. Sun filtered through the regularly spaced trees and dappled the exteriors of the stone buildings. The breeze from the nearby Seine swirled down the street, kicking up leaves.

Raya wandered in the direction of the nearest Métro station and found a bustling cafe filled with Parisians. She stood on the sidewalk and stared, unsure whether to approach the bar or take a seat at one of the tables.

Jet lag didn't help with clear thinking.

She swayed a little, made up her mind, and stepped up to the bar.

The bartender addressed her in French.

Raya pointed to the largest mug she could see and said the phrase she'd been practicing all morning: "*Bonjour. Un café, s'il vous plaît.*"

The drink arrived piping hot, steam curling from the top and tickling her nose as she leaned forward to inhale the scent.

Hallelujah. Rocket fuel at last.

She drank carefully at first, then faster and faster as it cooled. She tilted the cup at a precarious angle and knocked back the last few precious drops, then dropped the cup onto the bar with a satisfied clatter and turned to go.

As she turned, she caught sight of the man standing next to her at the bar.

In the front pocket of his tweed jacket, peeking out where a normal man might carry a pen, a crystal glittered and winked.

Raya gasped. Witches were so rare back home that it was shocking to just run into one here, as if witches were common.

The man glanced at her. The morning light glinted on his heavy-framed eyeglasses as his dark eyes assessed her. He didn't smile.

"I'm sorry! I didn't mean to stare. I'm just not used to running into"—she tilted her head to show him the wand tucked into her hair—"one of us."

He shifted his standing position to face her. His hands slid into the pockets of his jacket as he leaned one patch-covered elbow on the bar.

Watching his face was like watching the wheels turn in an intricate machine. She could almost hear the clicking whir of his thoughts.

"One of us?" His voice remained carefully neutral.

His cool response froze her friendly smile, but she soldiered on. "Are you here for the convention?"

Amusement flickered in his eyes, but no trace of it touched the rest of his smooth complexion. "What convention?" His words fell like flat stones.

Impulsively, Raya stuck out her hand. "I'm Raya, by the way."

He waited a beat before taking her hand. "Raya."

Their auras of power intersected.

His imperturbable mask didn't slip, but he must have reassessed her. "I'm Nathan."

The caffeine had finally kicked in enough for her to notice the time. "I better run, Nathan. Don't want to miss the opening presentation."

He smirked. "Neither should I."

Raya looked back just before exiting and saw him sipping his coffee and watching her with an expression that bordered on calculating. She could almost hear the gears turning in his mind. She shook off the strange impression and left, her quickened steps taking her to the station in record time.

The Paris Métro carried her swiftly to the convention center, a sprawling complex fronted with windows mounted at odd angles that flashed the sun's reflection in myriad directions. Signs for the "Natural Health Expo"—the convention's cover identity— decorated the entrance hall.

Raya hurried through the corridors to the main presentation room.

She'd never seen so many witches in her life. Hippie witches swept by wearing long skirts and yards of necklaces. City witches tucked sleek wands into structured bags as they clicked through the halls on stylish heels. Tattooed witches wore their designs proudly with skin-baring fashions. Wands, amulets, and charms galore adorned the attendees.

Raya planned to stock up. Just the thought of going shopping in the vendor hall filled her with avaricious delight.

A witch wearing a color-coded lanyard and carrying a palm-sized crystal stopped her just inside the entrance to the hall. "Wand, please," he said.

Raya's hand went automatically to her hair. "My wand?"

"Security check. We don't want to let the general public in, do we? Hold it out and begin a spell."

Raya pulled out her wand and concentrated, calling up the same spell she'd used on the airline representative at the baggage claim.

The other witch's crystal flickered. "You're all set." He looked to the next witch.

Now to find a place to sit. "Excuse me." Raya squeezed past a group of witches in jaunty coordinating "Support Your Local Coven" t-shirts and slid into an open seat.

The cavernous hall filled completely as the remaining attendees passed the security check.

Raya shifted in her seat and drummed her fingers on her knees before deciding to nibble on a leftover macaron from her bag while she waited.

The house lights dimmed and a musical fanfare rose in volume as the voice of an unseen announcer rippled over the crowd. "Please welcome to the stage: your master of ceremonies, the author of *Witching Into the Dark*, Nathan Lorde!"

A man in a tweed jacket walked onto the stage.

Raya choked on her macaron and coughed uncontrollably.

Nathan. Nathan from the coffee shop. She could have picked the brain of one of the top witches in the world, and instead she'd rushed off to catch a train.

Her dog-eared copy of *Witching Into the Dark* didn't have an author photo.

Raya kicked the leg of the seat in front of her in frustration.

Luckily, its occupant was too enraptured to notice.

Nathan removed his wand from his pocket and held it up in the palm of his hand. He closed his eyes and held his other hand, fingers loosely spread, over the wand.

A susurration rippled through the crowd before the gathered witches fell completely silent.

Light traced around Nathan, crisscrossing with geometric precision, forming a delicate filigree outlining a figure with a pointed top and a four-legged base.

The Eiffel Tower, made of light.

Raya's mouth fell open and a heady feeling of longing swept through her. The illusion demonstrated raw power as much as beauty.

He picked up the wand with his free hand like he was handling a very large bubble he didn't want to pop. He eased the wand away from the illusion with a gentle flick, sending the glowing tower floating over the center aisle.

Heads turned to follow the movement.

Raya hastily tugged her wand free and quietly aimed it at the illusion, determined to make up for the lost opportunity at the coffee shop. There were so many ways to do this wrong, and only one chance to get it right.

Gently, delicately, she asserted her concentration on attracting the light. She felt the spell catch, and immediately had to tamp down the impulse to pull harder.

Softer, Raya, softer.

The tower drifted closer.

She didn't dare look away to see if Nathan was watching. She brought it to herself, letting it float above her, knowing full well that its light would illuminate her where she sat.

Nathan's voice broke the silence. "I knew we were coming to the Eiffel Tower. I never guessed one of us would make the Eiffel Tower come to them," he deadpanned. He banished the light with a wave of the hand.

The audience broke into applause.

Had he seen her? Did he approve? Raya shook with adrenalin as butterflies did barrel rolls in her stomach.

4

Raya flung herself backward onto the bed, sending pillows flying. She stared up at the ceiling as her thoughts whirled. What a day!

She rolled over and reached for her bag, pulling out pages upon pages of notes she'd taken during the presentations. Little freebies from the vendor hall spilled out and rolled across the covers. Raya corralled the miniature bottles, crystals, and swatches into a pile.

A knock at the door interrupted her efforts.

"Hang on." Raya pushed up from the bed and padded over to the door. "Who is it?"

"*Ton pire cauchemar.*" Phoenix's unmistakable English accent came through even in French.

Raya unlocked the door and opened it partway. "What the hell is that supposed to mean?"

"Haven't you learned any French yet?"

"Can't you just fade through the door?"

"Did you want me to? Should that become our regular thing? Me popping into your hotel room unannounced?" Phoenix leaned into the doorway.

Raya rolled her eyes. "Get in here and stop making a spectacle of yourself."

"Oh, if I were going to make a spectacle of myself, you'd know it." He strolled to the bed. "What's all this?" He scooped up a handful of the convention swag.

"Put that down!"

Phoenix dropped the items. "Calm down. I'm not stealing your trinkets. I was just curious." He managed to look simultaneously hurt and haughty.

"Don't pout." Raya faced the mirror and fluffed her hair. "I was all set to be shown a good time."

"In those clothes?"

"Why should I change when all you ever wear is a heap of black topped with a leather jacket?"

"Touché." He loomed over her in the reflection. "Maybe I should get you one to match."

Goodness, he was tall. And annoying. She was going to call his stupid bluff. "Maybe you should." She turned around and shoved his chest, but he didn't budge. She changed tactics and pointed her finger at him. "Go ahead. Get me a leather jacket."

"Get you a leather jacket?"

"You suggested it."

An odd look passed over Phoenix's face. "I was only kidding."

Raya snickered. "Too bad. Maybe you should think before you speak, demon."

"Right. Well." Phoenix looked uncharacteristically lost.

"What's the matter? Cat got your tongue?"

"You want me to find you a leather jacket in Paris in July? Don't you want to go sightseeing or eating or whatever it is that lunatic mortals like yourself do in Paris?"

Raya sat down on the edge of the bed and regarded Phoenix. "Oh, Phoenix. How will you ever learn that you should never, ever, try to bluff me?" She tilted her head and smiled. "Unless you want to suffer the immediate consequences. Now let's go shopping."

She hopped up and swept out of the room without looking back to see if he would follow.

He followed—probably just to make sure she wouldn't have the last word. "Obviously you know where you're going."

"Obviously." For once, she actually did know where she was going, since she'd passed their destination on her morning walk to the train station.

They emerged from the hotel lobby into the late summer twilight. A short walk down the sidewalk, past the cafe, and across the Rue de Babylone brought them to the doors of the famous Parisian department store, Le Bon Marché.

"Voilà!" said Raya.

"Oh, very clever," said Phoenix. He pulled open the door and allowed her to precede him.

Raya breezed past. "Such a gentleman. Or should I say gentledemon?"

"Don't push it."

Raya laughed and ran ahead to a massive display of grapes piled in wicker baskets. "Look at these!" She reached out with both hands.

Phoenix darted after her and grabbed her hands. "You're not supposed to touch them unless you plan to buy them."

"So it's forbidden fruit?" His hands felt very warm wrapped around hers. She wriggled away and pretended not to be affected. "I didn't want to buy it. I just wanted to see your reaction. Where do they hide the jackets, anyway?"

"In July? Probably in the basement. Only you would want something so out of season."

Raya walked further into the store. "Oh, I don't know. Nathan Lorde was wearing a tweed jacket today."

"Nathan who? Never mind. He's probably some boring witch. Forget I asked."

"Nathan is the author of my very favorite witchcraft book and I met him at a cafe this morning—"

"How fascinating," Phoenix said in a tone that indicated the exact opposite.

"—and he made this Eiffel Tower made of light and I pulled it over so he would notice me and then he talked about the theory of magic—"

Phoenix rolled his eyes. "And did he?"

"Did he what?"

"Notice you."

"I think so."

"You're an attention-seeking missile, you know that?"

Raya picked up a bottle of cologne from a nearby counter and spritzed him. "Takes one to know one."

He waved the cloud of scent away. "How much coffee have you had today, anyway?"

"I lost count. As I was saying—oh, look!" Raya seized a distressed denim jacket from a nearby rack and held it up.

"Back away from the denim."

Raya dropped it back on the rack. "Spoilsport."

Phoenix caught the attention of a salesperson. "*Excusez-moi, avez-vous des vestes en cuir?*"

The salesperson responded in French and pointed deeper into the store.

Phoenix took the lead as they meandered through one exquisite room after another, until they reached a quiet department decorated with warm blond wood and flattering spotlights.

"She said there were a few left back here." Phoenix veered away to a rack set into one of the wooden displays. "Ah, here we are." He pulled a few forward and glanced at Raya, eyeing her for size.

Raya pounced on a jacket with a fit-and-flare shape. "Come to mama." She ran her hands over the butter-soft leather, stopping when the tag at the cuff scratched her palm. She flipped it over to view the price. Her stomach dropped. She hastily placed the jacket on the rack. "I was only kidding, you know," she said flippantly. "Just yanking your chain. Let's go."

"What? And deprive myself the pleasure of making you wear a matching jacket? Not on your life, witch."

"Really, Phoenix—"

"Quiet." He held the jacket open behind her. "Where do you think I get my money from?"

"I haven't the slightest idea. We never really—talk?" She made the realization only as the words left her lips.

"That's because you're too busy trying to be clever. Put the jacket on."

She carefully slipped her arms into the jacket. It fit like a dream.

Phoenix bent and whispered in her ear: "I steal from bad people. They'll hardly miss it."

"Stealing is wrong," said Raya, without any conviction whatsoever—and utterly distracted by his voice so close to her ear.

He straightened up and patted her shoulder. "So is casting spells to make people do what you want. I'd say we're even."

"I don't cast—"

"Really? What about your little shenanigan at the baggage claim?"

"That doesn't—"

"Or the time you conjured a demon and made him follow your friend's ex-husband all over creation?"

Raya whirled around to face him. "I didn't mean to conjure you, specifically."

He smirked. "Didn't stop you from threatening to make me do your lawn work, did it?"

"I—"

"Relax," he interrupted. "I'm just winding you up." He turned her around again by tugging strategically on the jacket, then slid it off her shoulders. "You really are easy to rile." He folded the jacket over his arm and sauntered off in the direction of the nearest cash register.

Left to fume among the racks of clothing, Raya didn't know whether to feel complimented or insulted by the comparison between their respective moral failings.

Either way, she'd somehow ended up coordinating outfits with the most irritating demon she'd ever met.

5

Before bed, Raya rummaged through her collection of free samples from the convention, placing a concentration crystal, a wand-cleaning swatch, and a packet of herbal perfume aside before holding a tiny bottle of dream-enhancing lotion up to the light.

She turned the bottle this way and that, looking for a list of ingredients. The bottle appeared to be too small to include the ingredients on the label. Raya twisted the cap free and sniffed.

The lotion smelled of rosemary and mint, with a sweet trace of chamomile and something else she couldn't identify.

She tipped the entire contents of the bottle into her hand.

Where to put it?

Raya dabbed a little on her arms and legs, and patted the remainder on her neck for good measure. She could always buy more if it worked.

She placed the empty bottle on the nightstand and turned off the light, then moved to the window and pulled the curtain aside.

The moonlight illuminated the creamy stone exteriors of the buildings lining the street, giving them an ethereal appearance despite their solidity. She held her wand to the window and opened her free hand, concentrating on absorbing the light of the moon through her palm and her wand.

Raya let the curtain fall back into place. She crawled into the bed and laid her head on the square pillow.

She'd never shown any skill with lucid dreaming, despite plenty of reading on the subject. Her dreams tended toward the fragmented and abstract, more like impressions than anything coherent.

Demons, on the other hand, walked through dreams as easily as they walked through the waking world. Too bad the skill didn't rub off from hanging around Phoenix.

Why had he followed her to Paris, anyway?

Her thoughts slid into blackness as sleep vanquished her consciousness.

A fire appeared before her. She reached toward it, not in longing for warmth, but in desperation for the flames to go out.

Her belongings were burning in the pyre.

She could see the outlines of her books, their pages curling up as they burned to ash.

Lost in the logic of the dream, Raya plunged her hands into the fire, grasping at the books, her hands and arms struck by searing pain. She felt tears fall and heard them hiss into steam in the flames.

A door slammed, and the fire disappeared. She leaned against the door, pushing with all her might, knowing that it would never swing open for her again.

"Please," she said, pressing her hand against the door. "Mom? Dad?"

They would never open that door again.

Not for her.

Not after they'd thrown her books into a fire in the backyard.

Raya screamed and the world shook, reverberating with rage.

She'd show them. She'd become the greatest witch ever known. It wouldn't matter anymore that she'd been thrown out of the house and disowned by her own family, not when she could command powers beyond their understanding.

The dark scene dissolved, replaced by a forest of tall trees punctuated with massive boulders.

Raya touched a tree trunk and felt the rough bark under her fingertips. Sunlight filtered through the canopy and danced across her skin.

Why was she here? What was happening?

Raya tossed and turned in the bed, the movement dragging her up from the depths of the dream like a swimmer buoyed to the surface of the water.

The cloying scent of the lotion suddenly repelled her.

She threw off the covers and staggered to the bathroom. The sight of her tear-streaked face in the mirror made her turn away in shame. She twisted the shower taps, removed her clothing, and stepped into the water before it was even warm, scrubbing the lotion away as fast as she could.

Never again.

The past was nothing but an ugly dream.

With every trace of the dream-enhancing lotion removed, she stepped out of the shower, dried off, and put her pajamas back on.

Still she shivered.

In the darkened hotel room, she reached for the new leather jacket she'd carefully hung in the tiny closet. She slipped it on over her pajamas, wrapped it tightly around herself, and curled up in the bed, her hands clutching the soft leather until the shivering subsided.

Oversleeping wasn't a great way to start the day. Raya felt like her feet were dragging through mud as she trudged into the convention hall. She'd skipped coffee to get there faster.

It was possibly the worst decision of her life.

Well, right after the decision to put on that damned dreaming lotion.

Raya shuddered.

What a disaster.

Determined to make the best of the day, she sought out the vendor hall. She'd stuffed her pockets with enough dollars and euros to make a sizable dent in the stock of any shopkeeper.

Magical supplies, after all, were far more important than groceries. She'd figure out how to continue eating when she got home to her real job as a school librarian. For now, she was going to spend her money like a sailor on leave—minus the excessive booze and questionable paid company.

Phoenix was the very definition of questionable company, but he certainly wasn't paid, and a few glasses of champagne here and there couldn't possibly be considered excessive.

Her self-justification firmly in place, she entered the vendor hall. Skirted tables and fabric booths stretched in long rows through the room. Raya hardly knew where to start, so she plunged into the nearest row, her head swiveling from side to side as she attempted to take it all in.

"Raya."

The voice over her shoulder, so clear and controlled that it cut through the ambient noise, sounded familiar. She turned. "Nathan."

Nathan crossed his arms. "That was quite a stunt you pulled at the opening presentation."

Raya made a snap decision to brazen it out against his appraising gaze. "Of course it was. How else was I supposed to get your attention?"

His thick eyebrows rose. "It worked."

"Not unless you tell me all your magical secrets. And skip the stuff in *Witching Into the Dark*—I have it memorized."

Nathan barked a short, bitter laugh. "I'm flattered."

Raya, sensing an advantage, barrelled on. "I haven't even gotten started yet. What you wrote about summoning—you wouldn't believe what I was able to do with it." Raya picked up a wand from the table they were standing next to and weighed it in her hand.

He blinked, once. "Go on."

Raya replaced the wand and drew him down the row of vendors by tugging on his jacket sleeve. "I had a real breakthrough. I encountered a demon, and boom! I banished him on the spot." She left out the part where she later tried to rescue the demon, and the other part where the demon fell in love with her friend, but those weren't the important parts.

At least, they weren't the parts Nathan should hear.

"That's very interesting," said Nathan.

Raya watched his eyes as if she could follow the strange clockwork of his thoughts.

When he spoke, it was stilted but sincere. "I wrote it with the intention of guiding witches to accomplish that sort of thing. It's gratifying to hear that it worked for someone."

Raya nodded eagerly. "And then, I was able to conjure another demon and command it to do my bidding." The fact that said demon's name was Phoenix and he was currently accompanying her on shopping trips to Le Bon Marché remained unsaid.

No need to clutter the conversation with useless details.

"Impressive."

Raya beamed. "Do you think so?"

His head tilted slightly as he appeared to be considering something, the motion almost birdlike when paired with his unblinking stare.

Raya held her breath so she wouldn't be tempted to interrupt his thoughts.

"I'm taking a side trip tomorrow. A little bit of magic-seeking," he said.

"You are?"

He nodded. "I already have an assistant, but…"

Raya's eyes widened hopefully.

"…we could use a third witch," he finished. "Would you be interested?"

Raya bit her lip and attempted to contain the wild glee bubbling up inside her. "Sounds very interesting. Where would we be going?"

"Hiking."

"Hiking?" She did not intend for the word to come out in a high-pitched squeak. Mother Nature's all well and good until a scorpion crawls up your pants. But Nathan was watching her, assessing her, and she had to be convincing. "Fantastic!" She pasted a smile on her face and hoped he bought it.

She would have suffered almost anything—scorpions included—for a chance to learn from the best.

"I'll leave a copy of the directions for you at the desk." He walked away without another word.

"Bye!" she called, doing her best to sound casual. She nonchalantly pivoted to the nearest table and grabbed the first thing she could lay her hands on, which turned out to be a book titled *How to Trap a Demon*. She flipped the pages without reading a word, waiting for Nathan to be out of sight.

When he was gone, she put the book down and did a happy dance in the aisle.

6

Phoenix wouldn't tell her where he was taking her that night, only that it was a secret and he'd have to blindfold her before they got there.

"So you finally decided to impress me?"

"I'm beginning to think the blindfold won't be enough. Maybe I should gag you, too," said Phoenix, brandishing a folded cloth.

Raya grabbed at it, but he pulled it out of reach.

"Behave, witch."

Raya subsided, her curiosity overwhelming the urge to tease the hell out of Phoenix.

"That's better. I could almost get used to you like this. I'll have to ply you with mysterious treats more often."

"You make me sound like a pampered dog. 'Sit, Raya. Wear this blindfold, Raya. Good Raya!'"

"That's how witches treat demons, usually."

Raya opened her mouth to fire off a retort, then shut it again. He wasn't entirely wrong.

"Speaking of obeying, you're going to have to follow a few rules."

"Rules?"

"Yes, rules. Rule one: you don't carry your wand."

"What—"

"Rule two: you don't make any sudden movements."

"But—"

"Rule three: you don't speak to anyone except me, and then only if you absolutely must."

"Are you serious?"

He shot her a look.

"You're serious," she said. She'd never seen him be serious about anything before.

They took the Métro away from the posh 7th *arrondissement* to a seedier neighborhood on the other side of the Seine, emerging from the station onto a sidewalk that was simultaneously wreathed in shadows and cut by the garish lights of neon signs.

Phoenix pulled her to the side and took out the blindfold.

She hesitated. "Phoenix, isn't this a little weird? Putting on a blindfold and walking down the street?" Their interactions were all fun and games—until now. Banter, she could handle. Trust was another story.

"Are you afraid?"

She couldn't read the faint edge in his tone, which made her even more nervous. Her lips pressed together. "Of course not," she lied. Her skin prickled with goosebumps. This was nothing like their usual flippant exchanges. This was different, and it was making her uneasy.

She snatched the blindfold from his hands and positioned it over her eyes. "Let's do this." She felt his hands at the back of her head tugging the wand out of her hair.

He took the ends of the blindfold and tied them.

She couldn't see. She felt his arm slip around her waist.

The leather they both wore slid together as they touched.

"Ready?" he said.

She nodded.

They walked side by side for a considerable distance. The noise of the passersby and the nearby clubs seemed amplified to the point of distortion.

Raya's disorientation and apprehension increased.

A heavy-sounding door creaked. Raya stumbled over the threshold. The door closed behind her and muffled the sounds of the street.

"Stairs," said Phoenix.

"You have to be kidding." She reached her foot out and bumped a stair.

"One foot in front of the other."

She took a hesitant step. "Is this where I get murdered?"

"Now would be a good time to practice rule three."

They made it up the stairs. Another door creaked open, allowing the sounds of clinking glass and laughter to filter out to the landing where they stood. They crossed a second threshold and the room, whatever it was, fell completely silent.

Phoenix removed the blindfold. "Remember the rules," he whispered.

Raya opened her eyes.

Demons.

Demons everywhere.

Some had tiny, delicate horns protruding from their heads. Others displayed massive feathered wings in a range of colors. Most were human-like demons with the appearance of male, female, or non-binary gender, but a few demons chose to look more traditionally demonic than human.

One demon looked like a combination of every nightmarish demonic trait humans had ever imagined: fangs, yellow eyes, ram's horns, and muscles like oversized ropes.

All of them stared at her without speaking.

Raya's mouth went dry.

Phoenix's wings, the color of red velvet cake, unfurled behind him with a sound like two umbrellas opening. "Just play it cool." He took her arm and led her toward the marble-topped bar.

The largest and scariest-looking demon blocked their path and addressed Phoenix with a rumbling growl. "Who said you could bring one of them here?"

"Back off, George," said Phoenix. "Cosmo says it's okay. Isn't that right, Cosmo?"

A petite demon in a midriff-baring top and a tiny pair of shorts leaned over the bar. "That's right. You got a problem with that, George?"

George hunched, making himself look smaller. "No problem, Cosmo."

"Why don't you buy the lady a drink and make up for your rudeness?" Her blunt-cut bob swayed as she tilted her head.

He shambled over to the bar and laid down some ancient-looking coins. "Pardon me, miss," he said to Raya.

"No problem," croaked Raya, before remembering she wasn't supposed to speak and clapping a hand over her mouth.

Cosmo glanced at her and began polishing a glass. "I bet he gave you a whole speech before he brought you here."

Raya, unsure of whether to respond, looked back and forth between Phoenix and Cosmo.

"Let me guess," Cosmo said, setting the glass down. "Don't talk, don't move, don't even breathe unless he says so."

"Cosmo—"

"Shut up, Phoenix."

Raya liked Cosmo more every second.

"He thinks he's so funny, scaring the daylights out of people. Like we're going to eat you." She poured a small amount of emerald-green liquid into two glasses and topped each one with a slotted spoon and a sugar cube.

Raya shot Phoenix a questioning look.

He held up his hands. "I was just trying to be careful."

"Since when have you ever been careful?" asked Raya.

"Must be a new thing," said Cosmo. She slid the glasses under the spouts of an odd fountain-like contraption that appeared to be filled with ice water. She turned the taps and water dripped out, drop by drop, onto the sugar cubes, through the spoons, and into the glasses. "Besides, you witches pose more danger to us than we do to you. By far."

"So why'd you let me come?"

Cosmo shrugged as she placed the green bottle on the shelf. "I trust Phoenix."

Raya scoffed. "This demon right here? Are we talking about the same Phoenix?"

The bartender smirked. "You must have trusted him if you let him drag you through the streets of this neighborhood blindfolded."

"Aha!" said Phoenix. He laughed. "She's got your number."

Raya opened her mouth to respond with a cutting remark, but became distracted as the liquid in the glasses slowly transformed from clear emerald to milky green. "What's it doing?"

Cosmo followed her gaze. "The pure absinthe is mixing with the cold water and sugar. The reaction changes the opacity of the solution." She reached over and twisted the taps closed. "That should be about right." She placed one glass in front of Raya and the other in front of Phoenix.

Raya lifted the glass and sniffed. The drink smelled of woody herbs.

"Now face each other and lift your glasses."

"Cosmo, really—" said Phoenix.

"Do this wrong and you'll have seven years of bad luck, so stop interrupting and pay attention. Now, look into each other's eyes." Cosmo's eyes glittered in the warm light as she watched the two of them.

Raya lifted her gaze from the drink to meet Phoenix's gaze. She'd never held his gaze longer than a second or two.

This was awkward.

Were those flecks of gold hidden in his deep brown eyes?

"*À votre santé*," he said.

"Try again, Phoenix," said Cosmo.

Phoenix lowered his glass and shot Cosmo a look.

Her serene expression, reminiscent of the Mona Lisa, left Raya wondering what on earth was wrong with what he'd said.

He looked at Raya and raised his glass again. "*À ta santé.*"

"Now you say '*À la tienne.*'"

Raya raised her glass to Phoenix and mimicked the sounds to the best of her French-speaking ability, which wasn't much, but it would have to do.

"Drink," said Cosmo.

Raya lifted the glass to her lips and took a sip of the drink. Strong and sweet, it raced past her lips like cold fire. "Oh, my."

Cosmo started setting up a drink for another patron. "Strong, isn't it?"

Raya cleared her throat. "You could say that."

Phoenix watched her. "So, what do you think?"

"I'm allowed to speak now?"

"Within reason."

Raya hesitated before speaking. "I'm impressed."

He slapped the bar. "Hell's bells. Finally, I get the better of you."

"Don't let it go to your head."

"Too late." He sipped his drink with an air of self-satisfaction, never breaking eye contact.

Warmth blossomed over her skin as she took a second sip.

7

Recovery from a night of absinthe and demons required a recharge in more ways than one. First, coffee and pastries. Then a few more pastries.

Then to recharge her wand.

Phoenix had pocketed her wand during the previous night's outing, leaving her unable to pick up stray currents of magic in the demons' secret gathering place, which was just as well—if she'd tried to absorb their power, they'd most likely have thrown her out, or worse.

Luckily, there was more than one way to recharge a wand. Moonlight and sunlight could be picked up just by wearing the wand in her hair. Other methods required a more oblique approach. There were reasons she'd spent years crashing weddings—events that inspired love, laughter, and tears were more than just emotionally charged.

They were magically charged, too.

In Paris, however, with her utter lack of language skills, she'd be unlikely to pass unquestioned, leaving Parisian wedding-crashing off-limits.

One way to recharge a wand—if you could pull it off—was to draw on the ambient power of artifacts, or works invested with great creative power. With dozens of museums within easy walking distance, Raya felt spoiled for choice.

She'd selected the nearby medieval museum for the sheer age of its collection. The fact that it sat atop an ancient Roman bath, one of the oldest sites in Paris, made it even more appealing. Raya checked the map in her hands, reorienting herself as she chose between turning onto a side street or continuing straight ahead before resuming her walk.

She recognized the museum by its steep roof and tiny turrets, which peeked over a castle-like wall enclosing the courtyard. To her relief, entrance to the museum required no conversation with the attendant. She paid the minimal fee with a few wrinkled bills and proceeded into the exhibits.

The trick would be twofold: to find the best sources of power, and to quietly absorb enough to recharge her wand without tipping off any nearby witches. Everyone did it, but it didn't pay to draw attention to yourself while doing so.

The room of stained glass stopped her in her tracks. The jet black walls and low lighting made the glowing glass appear to float in midair. She gazed up at one of the circular pieces depicting a red-faced demon abducting a woman. A smile slid across her lips as she caressed the wand in her hair, delicately encouraging it to take in the sparkling light.

Oh, the irony.

Feeling the magic of the art prickle her skin, she turned her gaze to other pieces. Most depicted men in states of sin or exultation. A stained glass angel drew her eye with his golden wings and an oversized flaming sword.

She could feel the touch of time on her shoulder, her lifespan a butterfly's in comparison to Phoenix and his immortal kin. Why did she allow him to stay near her even as his presence reminded her of her own mortality?

Perhaps it was because of his power. She'd summoned him, after all, and bound him to her will for a while, when she needed assistance—but those days were past.

Someday, when he became bored, he would leave her.

On closer inspection, the scenes depicted in the glass struck her as foreboding, even sad. Her stomach twisted.

Time to move on.

Raya entered the echoing rooms of the Roman bath. Her quiet footsteps took a meandering path to carvings of Jupiter, Vulcan, and the heavenly twins, Castor and Pollux. She lingered before the likeness of Cernunnos, the Stag Lord of the druids, before entering a room full of Christian altarpieces and sculptures.

So many millennia, so many beliefs. She touched the crystal on her wand and felt it tremble. The effort to draw lightly, to restrain from inhaling the latent power too fast and falling senseless on the floor, left her light-headed.

Gripping the guardrail, Raya paused to catch her breath before climbing the stairs to the final exhibit.

The narrow stairwell opened to a dimly lit circular room with strategically placed spotlights aimed on six massive tapestries.

Raya took a seat on the center bench facing the tapestries.

The vivid colors filled her vision. She removed her wand from her hair and set it in her lap, folding her hands over it as she concentrated on the tapestry panels.

The same woman appeared in each scene. Raya imagined herself in the woman's place, surrounded by the sumptuous details worked into each tapestry. In her mind, she touched the horn of the unicorn. She selected candies from a delicate serving dish and fed them to the parakeet that perched on her finger. The flowers in the lady's wreath were her own, filling her senses with their sweet scent.

Raya shuddered in ecstasy as the creative magic of centuries past trickled through her.

The final tapestry, and the most mysterious, featured the words *"À Mon Seul Désir"* written on the lady's tent, under which she held a jeweled necklace as she either removed it from its box—or put it away.

Raya took hold of her wand and stood, a little wobbly at first, to examine the tapestry closer. She read the plaque just off to the side.

According to the plaque, the meaning of the words remained a subject of debate.

To My Sole Desire.

What did she desire?

Was it the sparkling jewels she held in her hand? Or did "desire" refer to an unseen love?

Raya sought the truth of the tapestry from the magic it radiated, but as she coaxed the enchantment to reveal itself, it slipped away—leaving behind only the faint and silvery sound of a woman's laughter.

8

Raya stood in the plaza in front of the Eiffel Tower. The crowd swirled around her as she pivoted to each cardinal direction in search of Phoenix.

Where was he?

Late, of course. She regretted resolving to tell him about her upcoming field trip. It wasn't like he needed to know, anyway. But considering she didn't know a single soul in France, it probably wasn't a good idea to take off into the woods without letting someone know where she was going.

The Eiffel Tower loomed over her, taller and more massive than it appeared in photos.

She could almost feel the weight of it in her bones, a weight with its own gravitational pull.

"Well met, Your Witchiness," Phoenix murmured behind her.

She jumped. "Damn it, Phoenix. Stop sneaking up on me!"

"But it's so much fun."

"And you didn't even apologize for being late."

"You're right. I didn't."

She waited.

He crossed his arms and regarded her, a smile playing around the corners of his mouth.

"You're infuriating, you know that? I don't know why I let you follow me to Paris." She started walking, forcing him to jog to catch up, then rounding on him as he drew near. "For that matter, why did you follow me here?"

He put his hands in his jacket pockets and shrugged. "Because I was bored."

"You were bored? That's all?"

Phoenix stared at the Eiffel Tower. "Forever is a long time. You have to find amusement where you can get it." His gaze turned to her. "I suppose it's the same for you, isn't it?"

"Yeah, but my forever isn't as long as yours." Her hands clenched and released. She made a conscious effort to still them.

"I bet you won't be bored if I do this." He grabbed her by the hand and waist, then swept her into a mad waltz across the plaza.

"Phoenix—" She couldn't speak for laughing. "Phoenix, let me go!"

"Never! Or boredom will set in, and we can't have that." He dipped her so low her hair nearly touched the pavement.

"Don't you dare drop me."

"Or what?" He held her in the position as passersby parted around them like an island in the stream. "Will you bind me to your service forever? Make me do your lawn work and paint your toenails? Never let me go?"

She giggled helplessly.

He relented and pulled her upright. "See, you're not bored anymore. I told you, didn't I? When I want to make a spectacle of myself, you'll know it." He released her and walked away, toward the base of the tower.

This time, she had to jog to catch up. "I meant to tell you something."

He hummed a tune.

"You're not listening," she said.

"Were you saying something?"

"I'm leaving Paris for a day."

"Jolly good." He continued the tune by whistling.

"To meet Nathan and some other witches."

"Mr. Glowing Eiffel Tower? I have to say, I'm unimpressed. In fact, I'll do him one better. Watch this."

"Phoenix—"

"Wait for it."

"Are you listening to me at all?"

"And…now!" He snapped his fingers.

The Eiffel Tower lit up with flashing lights all over, as if swarmed by a thousand tiny paparazzi.

"You didn't do that," said Raya. "It's on a timer. It does that every hour."

"And yet"—he leaned in—"it's still more impressive than your new friend."

"It's better than I could do."

They walked on, slowly circling the tower.

"So what? Is that what you want? Drawing pretty lights in the air?"

Raya sighed. "It'd be a start."

"You have more power in your little finger than Nathan has in his whole body."

"No, I don't."

"So you're going to take lessons from him or something? Is that it?"

"We're going into the forest of Fontainebleau."

Phoenix stopped cold. "Why?"

"They're looking for a source of magic. He's letting me go with him."

"So you're going into the woods with some random witches."

Raya ignored the fact that he'd echoed her own private concern. "What are you, my mother?"

His eyes narrowed. "Far from it."

"Then try to understand, Phoenix. I live in a small town. I work as a school librarian. I don't even know any other witches. Everything I learned, I learned from a book. This is my chance to finally become the witch I've always wanted to be."

"So you get more powerful? Is that it? What does it matter?"

"I don't expect you to understand." She dug her fingers into her hair and tugged, the discomfort a distraction from the unease rippling through her.

"Maybe I don't understand because you don't bother to explain it to me."

"Who said I owed you an explanation?"

"You think because you can conjure me or banish me at will, I can't ask you a question?"

Holding eye contact in anger felt like channelling electricity through her body. "Why should I share anything with someone who's only going to hang around until he finds something better to do?"

Phoenix ran his hands through his own hair in a movement that mirrored hers. "Do you think I'm jealous? Is that what this is? I'm not jealous, you idiot—I'm worried."

She looked at him, thunderstruck. Phoenix didn't know the meaning of the word "worried."

His voice became softer. "Not all witches are like you. You know that. You know there are some who will go a lot farther to get what they want."

"I—"

"Just be careful." He turned and walked swiftly away into the crowd, fading into the darkness before she could stop him.

9

Verdant green fields flashed by as the regional train carried Raya through the French countryside on the way to the forest of Fontainebleau.

She rubbed the sleep from her eyes and shifted in her seat to lean her head against the window.

Sheer willpower had dragged her out of bed before dawn to catch the early train out of Paris.

It would be worth it.

The view flickered as the train passed through a forest, the rays of the rising sun piercing the trees like arrows of light.

At the station, she alighted on the platform and dodged the commuters who surged forward to board the train. She did not expect anyone to meet her, but it felt lonely all the same. Deciding she should save her feet for the hike ahead, Raya found a taxi outside the station and gave the driver the address of the cafe where she was to meet the rest of the group.

The city buildings—some old, some new—marched by as the little car made its way through the little city.

The driver pulled up alongside a cafe in the vicinity of the grand chateau of Fontainebleau.

Raya patted her hair and tugged her shirt straight before exiting the cab and stepping carefully onto the sidewalk. She peered through the windows in search of Nathan and his assistant, but saw no one she recognized.

Instead, a quiet contingent of townspeople started the day with mugs of café au lait.

Charming, but not quite the three-egg omelet she'd been hankering for, considering she needed a good, solid breakfast to start the day. Raya examined the menu board with the help of her phrasebook.

Fruit.

Toast.

Coffee with milk.

The French had style in spades, but they had a lot to learn about breakfast.

She settled for café au lait, examining the passersby through the window in hopes of spotting a familiar face. When more than half an hour had elapsed, a small amount of worry tickled her thoughts. She pushed it aside and waited another fifteen minutes.

No sign of Nathan.

Raya opened her bag and retrieved the directions he'd left for her at the convention, scanning the words that filled the page.

Yes, she'd taken the right train from Paris.

Yes, she'd gotten off at the right stop.

Yes, she'd found the cafe and had been waiting promptly at—

Raya slapped her forehead.

The instructions didn't say "7:00 a.m." They said "7:00 p.m."

The small amount of worry bloomed into a bouquet of concern. How could you go for a hike so late in the evening? No wonder she'd assumed the time meant early morning, not sunset. Nature was bad enough when you had plenty of light to navigate by, let alone when you were staggering around in the dark.

Perhaps it was a typo.

She read all the way to the bottom of the page and found the hotel where they were staying.

That settled it. She'd track them down and make sure she wasn't left behind, typo or not. A big breakfast would have to wait. Raya dug out the phrasebook and motioned to the waiter. "Bonjour, monsieur. Wait—hold on—I'll get it." She flipped the pages. "*Où est*—I know it's in here somewhere—"

The waiter regarded her with saintly patience.

"*L'hôtel! Où est l'hôtel?*" She pointed to the hotel information printed on the paper.

He peered at the paper, then unleashed a torrent of French accompanied by a complicated set of gestures.

"Slower, please." She rubbed her forehead. "Strike that. Can you draw a map?" Raya picked up a pen and squiggled it in the air.

"Ah!" he said. He flipped the paper over and drew a creditable map of the streets surrounding the cafe, carefully placing a star over her destination.

"Thank you! Merci!" She blew him a kiss and walked out of the cafe with a spring in her step.

While crossing the nearby square, the scent of fresh crepes wafted through the clean morning air. Raya found her footsteps veering toward the crepe stand without conscious thought.

Several stuffed crepes later, she followed the hand-drawn map to a hotel adjacent to the grand chateau. She did her best to look like she belonged as she crossed the lobby to a small outdoor garden with cafe tables, hoping she would discover the witches having breakfast.

No such luck. Her shoulders sagged as she considered her options. Would they really have left without her? Or was the paper correct, and the hike not scheduled to take place until it was nearly dark?

Surely it was too early to bother Nathan—but then, she'd come all this way.

She scribbled his name on the paper and carried it to the front desk. "Nathan Lorde?"

"You are friends?" the clerk asked in English.

Raya nodded enthusiastically and tried not to look like a serial killer.

"Your name?"

Raya gave her name.

The clerk picked up the phone and dialed. She said a few words in French, then switched to simple English. "You have a friend here." She paused. "Raya."

Seconds ticked by and sweat broke out on Raya's skin.

"He says go up."

They hadn't left without her. Raya thanked her lucky stars, then thanked the clerk and took the stairs two at a time to the second floor. She found the correct room and knocked on the door, anticipation curling around the crepes in her belly.

The door opened.

Nathan swung the door wide. "You're early," he said flatly.

A blonde-haired witch across the room squealed with delight and clapped her hands when she caught sight of Raya.

"I know, I'm sorry." Raya entered the room and jumped when the door banged closed behind her. "I misread the paper. I thought it said 7:00 a.m.—"

The blonde-haired witch flipped her smooth, blown-out locks over her shoulder and cast a teasing look at Nathan. "I told Nathan he should have been more clear."

"Raya, this is my collaborator—"

"I'm Lizzy!" She bounced out of her chair and gave Raya an impossibly cute hug.

Raya, not naturally a hugger, accepted the unexpected affection with a quick pat on the other woman's back. "Hi, Lizzy."

Lizzy drew back and looked at Raya with concern. "Have you eaten? You must have gotten up so early. I know—you can go with us!"

Raya refrained from explaining she'd already eaten. A second breakfast would probably do her good, considering the energy required for the hike, and she was not about to pass up the chance to have breakfast with two highly proficient practitioners. This was the kind of opportunity she'd been hoping for ever since she'd taken the first steps on the path of witchcraft.

"Go without me," said Nathan. "I'm not hungry."

Lizzy's eyes shone with disappointment, although Nathan didn't seem to notice. "Are you sure?"

Nathan turned away and picked up a book. "I'm sure."

"Just us girls, then!" Lizzy threaded her arm through Raya's.

Raya glanced back at Nathan to see if he'd picked up the false ring to Lizzy's overly bright tone.

He appeared to be fully engrossed in the book.

"Come on then," said Raya, tugging Lizzy out the door. She was sure she could fit at least one more croissant in before lunchtime.

They collected a few pastries from the lobby. Lizzy led the way out to the hotel grounds.

"Have you known Nathan long?" Raya nibbled the edge of the chocolate croissant. Best to take things slow.

"Absolutely ages," said Lizzy, gesturing with her beautifully manicured hand. The hot pink nail polish shone like it was wet.

"Are you—" Raya paused, unsure if she was being too blunt.

"Together?" Lizzy looked down at her plain croissant as if she'd find the answer in the flaky pastry. "Not for lack of trying on my part." She elbowed Raya and giggled. "Nathan's got so much going on. He's so busy, you know?"

Raya had never seen anyone pine so hard. "How busy can he be?"

Lizzy talked around a mouthful of croissant, but made it look adorable rather than ill-mannered. "Nathan is all about the work."

"The work?"

Lizzy waved her croissant in a gesture that encompassed the whole world. "The work. The power. Don't get me wrong"—she looked at Raya and a little line formed between her eyebrows—"I take my practice very seriously. But it's everything to Nathan. No time for silly little things." She laughed lightly. "Like love."

10

Raya faced the entrance to the forest with trepidation. The beautiful sunlit trees, edged with gold in the fading light of the evening, only reminded her of what they would look like without the sun's friendly illumination. Her gaze snagged on a fallen tree with the branches twisted outward like the outstretched fingers of a giant hand.

Lizzy bustled past carrying a bag full of gear. "Isn't this exciting?" she chirped.

Exciting was not the word. Terrifying, maybe. Raya felt profoundly ill-equipped. She'd come to France for a nice indoor convention—not a pitch-black ramble through an unfamiliar forest surrounded by whatever beasts inhabited such an environment.

Lions. Tigers. Bears.

"Oh, my," said Raya, adjusting the strap on her pack.

"What's that?" said Lizzy.

Raya shifted the weight on her back and checked her wand's position in her hair. "Nothing."

"Are you ready?" Nathan handed them each a hiking pole for extra stability in the darkness.

Lizzy swung the pole like a tap dancer. "Ready!"

Nathan led the way into the woods, his stiff posture loosening as he hit the trail.

The path unfurled before them, wide enough for two people to walk side by side.

Raya fell into step with Lizzy. She'd seen a map of the forest earlier, but the simple two-dimensional view didn't even begin to translate to the deep complexity of the surrounding landscape.

"We were so busy getting ready earlier I didn't get to ask you about yourself," said Lizzy.

Raya breathed heavier as the path went up a rise. She felt the pull of needing to share something about herself since Lizzy had been so open with her. "Did I tell you I was a school librarian?"

"No—really? That's so cool! And you picked up witchcraft all on your own?"

"Self-taught." Raya tried to breathe evenly but her exhalations came out in winded puffs. She hoped she didn't collapse before it was all over. "You?"

"My mom was a witch. She's kind of retired now, but she taught me a lot. I'm really good at sensing things."

"Sensing things?"

"Magic. Speaking of which, I was in the audience for Nathan's speech—did you know that?"

Raya shook her head.

"You lit up like a firecracker!"

Raya's thoughts whirled like fallen leaves in the wind. Her little stunt had been spotted not just by Nathan, but by his assistant. No wonder she'd received an impromptu invite on their field trip. Belatedly, she realized that Lizzy had been waiting for her to reply. "Thanks. I don't really have a particular thing that I'm good at, like you."

Lizzy smiled. "Are you kidding? You draw power like a magnet."

They walked on, the sounds of their footsteps punctuated by birdsong echoing in the trees.

"First landmark up ahead," said Nathan.

Boulders tilted over the path, corralling them into a dark and narrow opening.

Inside, Nathan planted his hiking pole in the dirt floor of the cave. "Welcome to the Grotto of Perjury."

Lizzy's musical laugh rebounded strangely off the stone walls. "Couldn't they come up with a better name?"

Raya placed her hand on the cool stone, faintly lit by the last remaining daylight. "Why is it called that?"

No one answered.

Nathan retrieved a granola bar from his pack. "If we stay here for a few minutes, your eyes will adjust to the darkness. You'll be able to see better."

Oddly, Raya wasn't hungry. The chill of the stones seeped into her skin, setting off goosebumps. She imagined herself wrapped in her new leather jacket, which she'd left behind to keep it safe. The thought brought a smile to her lips but did nothing to alleviate the cold.

Lizzy sat next to Nathan on a boulder, not quite close enough to touch, and delicately removed the burrs that had hitched a ride on her clothing.

He finished his granola bar and tucked the wrapper into his pack.

Outside, the darkness became complete.

They resumed the hike.

Despite knowing the forest contained nothing that hadn't been there an hour ago—when it was still light—Raya couldn't help flinching at unfamiliar noises. Without a hiking pole, she would have tripped more than once.

Her eyes adjusted. The forest itself appeared limned in moonlight, almost like a photo negative. The leaves rustled in the night breeze.

The path opened up to a clearing. In the center of the clearing, on a small rise, stood what appeared to be a miniature castle, its four turrets silhouetted against the night sky. A steep stone staircase led up to the castle.

Raya stopped at the bottom of the steps and stared up at the castle. "What is that doing here?"

"It's an observation point. Built about a hundred years ago." Nathan removed his pack and set it on the stair.

Lizzy placed her pack on the ground and knelt, stroking the stone stairs. "Rebuilt after it was destroyed."

"After an 'earthquake.'" Nathan made exaggerated quotation marks in the air, his voice dripping with sarcasm.

Lizzy shook her head slowly as she continued to run her hands over the stairs. "Not an earthquake." She smiled, her even white teeth glinting in the moonlight. "Come here, Raya."

Raya set her pack and hiking pole down and knelt next to Lizzy on the stairs.

Lizzy placed one hand on the step, then took Raya's hand and laid it over her own. "Feel it."

Raya felt the vibrant sparkle of Lizzy's magic through her hand. She closed her eyes and let Lizzy's hand conduct the magic hidden within the stones. Raya felt the power trickle through, and with it, a sense of what had happened long ago. She opened her eyes. "There were witches here before."

"Attempting the same thing we are." Despite the cold, Nathan removed his jacket and rolled up his sleeves.

Raya stood up. "But—the original structure—it was destroyed?"

"They lost control," he said. "We won't." He took a Swiss Army knife from his pocket. "We need supplies. Lizzy, set up, please." Nathan walked away and disappeared into the dark edge of the clearing.

Lizzy hopped down from the stairs and picked up her pack. "On it."

Raya looked up at the turrets. "It must have been a lot of power."

"Come on. Last one to the top's a rotten egg!" The blonde witch's hair bounced as she ran up the stone steps.

There was no way Raya was going to run up those stairs with a full pack. She trudged after Lizzy, reminding herself again that it would all be worth it.

From the top of the miniature castle, the forest lay below her like a carpet worked in shades of midnight. She turned away from the castle walls and found Lizzy laying out the tools of their trade. "Where's your wand?"

Lizzy shimmied a little and pulled a crystal-topped stick from under the neckline of her blouse. "Mama always said to keep it in a safe place."

Raya laughed despite herself.

Lizzy tucked her wand behind her ear like a stray pencil. "So here's what we're going to do. We're going to work together, like we did on the stairs. I'll hook into the source of the power, and you draw it out."

"Then what?" Raya imagined the amount of power it would have taken to collapse a building of this size.

"Nathan will direct it."

"Direct it where?"

"Into the wands." Lizzy wiggled hers. The crystal winked in the light of the moon.

Raya had never worked with another witch before. She would have to trust both of them to know what they were doing.

The sound of Nathan's footsteps carried from the direction of the stairs. He reached the top and surveyed the preparations. "Ready?"

"Almost." Lizzy lay on the floor, face-up, her arms slightly away from her body and her palms open to the sky.

Nathan took out a compass. "Can you orient your head here?" He gestured.

Lizzy scooted herself around to match his position.

Raya watched them. "Does the direction matter?"

"It does for this." He bent and checked Lizzy's position relative to the compass.

Lizzy looked up at him and smiled.

Raya frowned. "Why? I thought you were directing the magic into our wands."

"Most of it." He straightened. "I have a side project."

"Nathan always has a side project," said Lizzy.

"I have another power source I'm working on. If I can get a sighting on it from here, I might be able to track it down."

Lizzy clapped her hands. "Such fun!"

Nathan's lips pressed together. Clearly, he was done with chitchat. "Raya, kneel next to Lizzy."

Raya lowered herself to the floor.

Lizzy gave her a broad wink. "Here we go!" From her position lying on the floor, she flipped her hands palm down.

Nathan checked his watch and Lizzy's position one final time. "Put your hand over hers."

Raya touched the wand in her hair once, then laid her hand over Lizzy's. "When I draw the power, what do I do with it?"

"Imagine you're filling a hot air balloon above your head," said Nathan.

"And if something goes wrong?"

He cocked one eyebrow. "Don't let it."

Lizzy closed her eyes. A faint smile touched her hot pink lips.

Raya felt Lizzy questing for the signature of power lingering around them. Minutes ticked by as Raya knelt, her legs beginning to cramp, her hand sweating lightly on Lizzy's perfectly manicured fingers.

Lizzy gasped.

It was like striking a vein—a vein made of gold lava. A wave of nausea passed over Raya as the sheer size of it barrelled into her consciousness. To make a mistake while drawing on this source would be catastrophic. She was not prepared for this. Nathan should have told her. This was no artifact sitting quietly in a museum, to be lightly drawn on to replenish subtle magics. This was a power substation—no, a nuclear reactor—of pure, chaotic magic.

No wonder the original building had been blown to smithereens.

She'd be surprised if the witches hadn't been, too.

11

Her instincts screamed to slam shut the connection between herself and Lizzy. Time slowed as she braced herself against the floor with her free hand. The magic surged through, forging a sudden bridge between her and the other witches.

Lizzy's bright and bubbly facade cracked as if cleaved along a fault line. Sadness seeped through, laced with longing for Nathan.

Ambition radiated from Nathan, cold and pure like a Damascene sword. He had gambled on Raya's natural ability and her own hunger for power—and if she didn't destroy them all in the process, he would win the bet.

Raya's breath froze as she tried to balance the onslaught of the magic and the intrusive thoughts. Could they see into her mind, too?

She had to breathe.

She had to stay in control.

If she died, Phoenix would kill her.

She remembered the look on his face just before he left her at the Eiffel Tower.

Raya dragged a breath into her lungs. She would not fail. Not now. Not after everything she'd been through. Unbidden, the memory of the pyre of her belongings flashed to mind.

There was no going back. By her will alone, she would build a new life out of the shrieking chaos.

She drew upon the waterfall of power, drawing it through and away from Lizzy, holding it above them all.

His hands extended, Nathan split the burgeoning energy into four strands, directing one to each of the three witches and one into the distance.

The magic cascaded into her wand. She feared it would catch fire in her hair but didn't dare move. She used her enhanced power to push back on the wild magic like twisting a cap on a bubbling bottle of soda.

Raya withdrew her hand from Lizzy.

Lizzy clenched her hands into fists.

The witches gasped as one.

It was over.

Raya collapsed next to Lizzy, their exerted breathing ringing loudly in the stone room.

Nathan slid down the wall into an exhausted crouch, resting his head on his knees.

Raya tilted her head toward Nathan. "You could have told me this place was a powder keg."

He looked up. "Would it have stopped you?"

She knew the answer, and he did too.

Lizzy hauled herself up from the floor and stretched. "I could use a long nap and a steak. Maybe two steaks!" She reached her hand down to help Raya up.

Raya took it and swayed unsteadily to her feet.

Lizzy threw her arms around Raya. "We did it!"

Raya didn't have the energy to escape, so she stood there and let Lizzy squeeze her until the air in her lungs felt scarce.

Lizzy let go and gave Raya a teasing push. "And who was that handsome fellow?"

Nathan stood up. "I didn't see anyone handsome."

Lizzy giggled. "Quiet, you. Come on, Raya—dish!"

"Who?" Raya turned away and rummaged in her pack to stall for time.

"If you were thinking about him during all that, he must be pretty special." Her musical voice echoed in the night.

The last thing Raya needed was to reveal her demon acquaintance. "Just someone I met at the convention." Raya shrugged her pack onto her back, hoping Lizzy would let the subject go.

No chance.

"Good-looking witch in a black leather jacket? You better lock him down, girl."

Raya winced at the irony of Lizzy's assumption that Phoenix was a witch. "Well—"

"Oh! I know! You should bring him to the party at the end of the convention." Lizzy bounced up and down.

Raya felt the color drain from her face and thanked the universe it was still dark. "I don't think—"

"On the last night of the convention! Of course you should. Even Nathan is going." She pranced over to Nathan and mussed his hair.

"Not willingly." He allowed Lizzy's touch without showing any sign of noticing it.

Raya's gaze traveled between the two witches. What a weird dynamic they had. Her life would never be that complicated.

Not if she had anything to say about it.

The witches trooped down the stairs and into the woods. Disorientation, exertion, and lack of sleep took its toll—the dark forest emanated an unreal quality, made worse by the latent power leaking from their wands and spiraling away into the canopy.

A nap and two steaks sounded like a solid plan.

When they finally reached the edge of the forest, the witches faced each other.

Nathan, solemn as ever, said nothing. The streetlights lining the edge of the forest cast a yellow glare across his glasses.

"Thank you for inviting me," said Raya. It felt formal but appropriate, and she was too tired to come up with anything better.

"Where are you staying?" asked Lizzy.

"In Paris?"

"No, silly. Here."

"Oh." Raya hesitated. "I'm not. I took the train from Paris this morning."

"But it's the middle of the night! No trains are running now."

Raya opened her mouth to suggest she would find a McDonald's, or the French equivalent, that was open 24 hours, to wait for the trains to start running. She didn't get a single word out.

Lizzy threw her arms in the air. "Sleepover!"

"That's not necessary, really—"

Lizzy didn't let her finish. She hooked her arm through Raya's and skipped down the sidewalk.

Raya nearly fell over from the sudden movement. To regain her balance, she had to start skipping, too. The absurdity of the situation hit her full force. A laugh bubbled out, which set Lizzy off—and they both doubled over, laughing like madwomen.

Nathan observed them impassively. "Are you two finished?"

Raya wiped tears of laughter from her eyes.

Lizzy caught Raya's gaze and winked. "Come on, Nathan, you know you want to."

They rushed him as one, seizing his arms and very nearly dragging him until he gave up the fight and lifted his feet in a reluctant skipping motion.

⸻ ◆ ⸻

Raya settled into an upholstered chair in Lizzy's room, too tired to stand and too adrenalized to lie down.

Lizzy, who had disappeared into the bathroom, poked her head around the corner. "Are you going to sleep?"

"I don't think I can. I feel like I drank a pot of coffee."

"Good!" Lizzy bustled over, her hands full of something that clinked together as she carried them. She deposited two handfuls of nail polish bottles onto the table next to Raya.

"Don't you want to sleep?"

Lizzy fluttered her hands. "Can't. Whenever I handle that much power, I'm wired for hours. Might as well make the most of it. Which color do you like?"

"Me? I'm not much of a paint-your-nails person."

Lizzy continued to stare at her with hope in her eyes.

"But I guess I could go with this one." Raya picked up a red bottle.

"I love it! This is going to be so fun." She plopped into the other chair and reached across the table for Raya's hand. "So tell me all about your guy."

"He's not actually my guy." Raya's nerves fired up as she wondered what Lizzy could sense about her just by holding onto her hand. Then she got even more nervous when she thought about Lizzy sensing her nervousness.

She willed herself to calm down. It was only a manicure.

Lizzy shook the bottle and removed the cap. "I sense you have some strong feelings about him."

Damn it.

Raya laughed it off. "Strong feelings like annoyance, maybe."

Lizzy stroked a smooth coat onto one nail. "Really?"

Sweat broke out on Raya's forehead. Could you block another witch's perception? She had no idea. She'd never worked with witches before and she didn't dare try a spell now.

Nine nails to go.

"Because it doesn't feel like annoyance to me." Lizzy dipped the brush into the bottle and brushed the lacquer onto another nail.

Raya swallowed. "No?"

Lizzy blithely stroked a coat of polish onto the next nail. "It feels like fear."

Raya almost tore her hand out of Lizzy's gentle grasp.

Lizzy painted the ring and pinkie finger nails with two quick swipes. "That's one hand done."

Raya did not want to put her other hand in Lizzy's.

She had to put her other hand in Lizzy's.

Lizzy took it and applied polish slowly and carefully to the first nail. "Not that you're afraid of him, but that you're afraid of what he is to you."

It took every ounce of Raya's restraint not to snatch back her hand and run out the door.

Lizzy didn't look up as she painted the next nail. "Am I wrong?"

Could she lie? How could she lie when she didn't even know the answer to the question? "I don't know."

Four nails to go.

Now Lizzy looked up, her eyebrows lifted. "You don't know?"

"I guess I never thought about it."

Which was true.

Lizzy dipped the brush and painted the next nail. "This color looks good on you."

Raya looked at the red shade on seven of her nails. It certainly made an excellent symbol of the panic blaring in her brain. "Maybe I should get a red dress for the party." Maybe, if she mentioned dresses, Lizzy would stop going on about hidden feelings.

"I see you wearing black." Lizzy painted another nail. "And"—here she paused to reload the polish on the brush—"I see him wearing black, too."

Raya twitched as Lizzy painted the last two nails.

Lizzy tilted her head and smiled as she released Raya's hand. "See? I told you this would be fun."

12

Raya scooped up a large bouquet of roses from the florist's stand and buried her face in the red petals. They matched her nails. If Lizzy hadn't fallen asleep, she probably would have attempted to paint Raya's toes, too, just to have an excuse to get more details about Raya's mystery man—who wasn't a man at all—and, for that matter, wasn't Raya's, either.

She'd barely managed to slip away to catch the first train of the morning back to Paris while Lizzy slept.

A few café au laits would remedy the effects of a sleepless night, for now.

Belatedly, she remembered that touching an item signaled intent to purchase. Her gaze traveled up from the red roses to the shopkeeper, who fixed her with a pointed look.

She owed herself a treat after such a long night, didn't she?

Raya dug in her pockets for enough money to purchase the bouquet.

The shopkeeper's expression became much sunnier as he wrapped her purchase in paper, tied it with a bow, and handed it back to her.

Raya hugged the bouquet and continued down the sidewalk. At her hotel, she greeted Ahmed, the hotel clerk, with a cheery wave of the roses, and continued upstairs to stash them in her room.

Only when she reached her room did she realize she had no vase. She briefly considered filling the small trash can with water, then settled on stoppering the bathroom sink and propping the cut ends of the flowers in the water.

She had almost left the bathroom when a thought struck her. Why not use the minor summoning she'd learned at the convention to contact Phoenix? Whereas a major summoning was like lassoing someone against their will, a minor summoning was no more intrusive than calling someone on the phone.

Surely he wouldn't mind.

She turned back to the sink and tore all the petals from one rose.

Where to cast the spell? She didn't dare ruin the carpet, so the hotel room floor was out of the question. Raya evaluated the amount of space around the sink and decided it would suffice. She retrieved her spellcasting supplies, consecrated the tiny area with her wand, then built the altar according to the requirements of a minor summoning, arranging the rose petals around it.

She carefully lit the candles and took a cleansing breath. The extra power vibrating through her set her head spinning. She steadied herself against the sink and concentrated. "Phoenix," she whispered, attempting to harness the power without allowing it to blast through her uncontrolled.

Unlike the first time they'd met, when her summons had dragged him unwillingly away from some sort of debauched party, this time he would come—or not—as he chose.

Nothing.

She breathed the fragrance of the rose petals and tried again. "Phoenix."

Still nothing.

Fickle demon. Leave it to Phoenix to refuse to answer the metaphorical phone. It would have been easier to simply cast the major summoning and call him up whether he wanted to show or not. "Third time's the charm," Raya muttered. "Phoenix!"

The candles extinguished themselves, plunging the room into darkness. Raya instantly felt a presence behind her.

"Did you summon me into a bathroom, witch?"

Raya hastily reached for the light switch. Light flooded the room, revealing Phoenix, who cocked a haughty eyebrow at Raya's reflection in the mirror.

"I'm sorry—did you have somewhere else in mind?"

Phoenix's mouth went slightly agape. "No—"

"Then don't criticize." Raya slid past him and out of the bathroom.

He followed, folding his dark red wings away. "You smell like a magic forest fire." He wrinkled his nose and fanned the air. "What did you do out there? I could feel the blast all the way from here."

"I got more magic."

"That's it? That's all you have to say about it?"

"It is until I get something to eat. A steak, preferably. My treat."

"Your treat? Are you ill?"

"No, I'm just hungry."

"Well, I don't eat. So that's not much of a treat." Phoenix sat on the bed and crossed his arms.

Raya took her jacket from the closet and put it on. "No? You drink, though. Like a fish, as I recall."

Phoenix sprang up. "Now you're talking. How about a *brasserie*?"

"I don't need a bra, Phoenix. I need a steak."

He rolled his eyes. "Not a brassiere, you philistine. A *brasserie*: a restaurant that serves beer, bread, steak, and fries."

Raya laughed. "Oh! In that case, lead the way."

<hr>

Mirrors covered nearly every wall of the neighborhood *brasserie*, making it almost impossible to judge the size of the restaurant at a glance. Brass fixtures, white tablecloths, and dark wood completed the old-school Parisian look.

Raya slid into a seat on the leather banquette, while Phoenix took a chair across the table.

The waiter delivered the printed menus and left them to examine the choices.

Phoenix tossed his menu on the table.

Raya peered at the French words. "Which one is a steak?"

Phoenix smirked. "You'll never guess."

She shook the menu as if airing a sheet. "Yes, I will. Let's see—oh." Her finger landed on the French word for steak.

It was "steak."

He chortled as the realization hit her.

Raya picked up her napkin and whipped him with it. "Very funny."

When the waiter returned, she ordered *steak frites* and a glass of champagne.

Phoenix ordered only a *bière*.

"Why don't you order some food? I know you can eat."

"Eating is weird." Phoenix waved his hand negligently. "And human."

"And drinking's not?"

"I choose to ignore the contradiction."

Raya snorted. "Denial isn't just a river in Egypt."

He leaned forward and rested his elbows on the table, cradling his face in his hands. "Tell me more about this so-called 'denial' of which you speak. Does it have anything to do with hanging out with a demon while also avoiding letting your witchy friends know about it?"

The waiter delivered their drinks.

Raya took a sip of champagne. "I'm not in denial."

"That is a classic example of denial."

"Shut up."

He took a drink of beer and smacked his lips. "You're a great big ball of contradictions and denial."

"And what does that make you?"

Phoenix shrugged. "You tell me, Witchiepoo."

Raya set her glass down with a thunk. "You're just an immortal trust fund kid with the attention span of a squirrel."

"You wound me." He pressed his hand where his heart would be, if he had one. "My attention span extends for minutes—nay, hours." He cocked his head. "How long have I been putting up with you, anyway?"

"You're the one who followed me to Paris."

"I? Followed you? I was visiting Paris before your umpteenth grandsire was born."

"And your latest trip just happened to coincide with mine?"

Phoenix swallowed a gulp of beer. "I was bored."

Raya threw her hands up. "And there we have it. You were bored."

"What do you think it's like, being an immortal supernatural being? I've seen it all. I've done it all. Now I just—wait."

"For what?"

"I don't know!" He caught her gaze across the table, his eyes troubled. "What would you do?"

"Me? Travel, I guess."

"But what if you've already been everywhere?"

"Study? Learn something?"

"For what?"

Raya shrugged. "Just for the joy of it, I guess?"

"The 'joy' of it palls, I can tell you, after a few thousand years."

The waiter delivered Raya's platter of food, piled high with steak and french fries and emanating a heavenly smell.

"Mmm. Smell that." Raya leaned over the plate and inhaled.

Phoenix wrinkled his nose.

Raya cut slices from the steak and examined the doneness. "Perfect."

"If you ask for ketchup, I'll pretend I don't know you."

"I already pretend I don't know you. So we'll be even." She popped a slice of steak in her mouth, followed by a fry.

"I don't see what the big deal is, anyway." He eyed the steak.

She waggled a slice on a fork at him.

He snatched it and bit into the steak like a reluctant child. Chewing thoughtfully, he handed her the empty fork. "Not bad." Then he stole a fry.

"I thought you didn't eat."

"I don't." He stole another fry.

"Are you saying that being a demon is boring, essentially, because you don't die?"

Phoenix finished the fry and swallowed. "Well, aren't you an uplifting dinner companion?"

She ignored the sarcasm. "I mean, I know I'm going to die someday. So I go to Paris, I eat steaks and drink champagne, and I become the best witch I can possibly be, because I have a timer hanging over my head."

He stole two fries.

She shielded her plate with her hands. "Get your own, demon."

He stuffed both of the stolen fries in his mouth with a rebellious air. "What am I supposed to do?"

Raya pointed her knife at him. "I'm not telling you to do anything. But for someone who doesn't have to worry about dying, you sure don't seem to be doing much living."

For once, he seemed to be at a loss for a comeback. Instead, he picked up a fry and pressed it to her lips in a shushing motion.

She bit it and grinned. Point scored.

13

The last day of the convention required hard choices as Raya crammed everything she possibly could into her workshop schedule. When the line for "Supernatural Summonings: Binding and Banishing for the Advanced Witch" stretched all the way down the convention hall, virtually guaranteeing she wouldn't get in, she detoured to "Macaron Magic: An Introduction to Kitchen Spellcraft" instead.

After all, she'd done pretty well with binding and banishing all on her own, considering she'd managed to bind Phoenix on the first try. She tried to picture binding Cosmo, or even George, to do her bidding, and had to brush away the uncomfortable thoughts like cobwebs. Those ideas were easier to swallow when you hadn't actually spent time with a demon—let alone toasted one with absinthe and shared a plate of steak frites.

But macarons and magic in the same workshop? Snacks and spellcasting in one fell swoop?

Talk about a win-win.

The meeting room contained a temporary kitchen set up in the front of the room with a large tilted mirror overhead. The macaron ingredients appeared in the reflection, along with an assortment of kitchen utensils, plus an additional tray of arcane ingredients and tools.

The show kitchen faced a long row of tables loaded with materials for the participants. Raya took a seat next to the table and eagerly examined the items on the table.

A woman in a chef's uniform—with a wand stuffed jauntily into the brim of her toque—stepped up to the kitchen set. She adjusted the microphone headset. "Is this thing on?" The sound boomed through the room. "I guess it is." She chuckled and adjusted something on the headset.

Raya leaned forward.

The chef smiled and continued. "So often we talk about putting love in our cooking. The secret ingredient is love, is it not? We think of this as a metaphor. But what if you literally put love into what you bake?"

One of the witches raised her hand. "You mean a love spell?"

"Not a love spell, exactly. By putting your heart into a recipe, you create a spell to unlock feelings. Does that make sense?"

The questioner nodded.

Raya wished she'd picked a different workshop, one that didn't involve unlocking feelings. She glanced discreetly over her shoulder.

The doors were already closed.

The other workshops in this time slot were surely full by now, anyway. She released a quiet sigh and returned her attention to the speaker.

"As I was saying, we will learn to incorporate our intentions into each step of the recipe, from handling the ingredients, to making the batter, to the baking process itself. Since we have already combined the almond flour and the sugar for you, let us begin by beating the egg whites to stiff peaks."

Raya reached for the bowl and the whisk, determined to do it well even if she didn't particularly want to do it at all.

***

While riding the Métro back to her hotel at the end of the day, Raya examined the paper sack filled with her handiwork: a dozen or so slightly misshapen macarons from the kitchen magic workshop. She didn't dare throw them away. She brought the bag closer and inhaled the scent. They smelled so delicious—even if they were a bit lumpy.

Surely one bite wouldn't hurt.

Yes, it would. She'd probably confess some deep, dark secret to the nearest Métro passenger.

Raya quickly stuffed them out of sight in her bag before she did anything she would regret.

Out of sight, out of mind. She'd figure out how to dispose of them later. Right now, she had to get ready for the party.

She hadn't brought anything fancier than her usual little black dress, an all-purpose garment she relied upon for just about any occasion. The leather jacket would dress it up with a bit of an edge.

She examined her nails. Lizzy's nail polish was remarkably tenacious. Perhaps she could pick up a red lipstick to match from Le Bon Marché.

Raya dropped off the day's swag, papers, and questionable baked goods in her hotel room before heading out on foot in search of a new lipstick.

The cosmetics clerk, despite not speaking any English, understood Raya's intention well enough after Raya pointed to her red nails and her lips several times. The contrast was obvious. The clerk pulled a sleek black case from a tray and demonstrated the color of several lipsticks with a quick swipe on the back of her hand.

When she found a close match to the nail polish color, Raya gave her a thumbs up.

The clerk rang up her purchase, and Raya left with her pockets lighter but carrying a pretty little shopping bag with her new lipstick tucked inside.

She opened the door to her hotel room to find Phoenix sprawled on the bed, his red wings flapping slowly as he changed channels with the remote. "Make yourself at home, why don't you?"

"Thank you. I will." He stopped on a program of French cartoons.

"You're watching cartoons, yet you call *me* a philistine?"

"Like I said, I choose to ignore the contradiction."

"Suit yourself. I need to shower and get ready for the party. Think you can behave yourself for a few minutes?"

He spared her a brief glance before returning his attention to the TV screen. "No."

Raya rolled her eyes and retreated to the bathroom with her outfit. She showered quickly and dressed, then set her unruly hair with a little extra mousse and a minute or two under the hair dryer. She applied the makeup she'd brought with her, then added the new lipstick as a finishing touch.

When she emerged, she found Phoenix still sprawled on the bed watching cartoons, but with crumbs all down his front and a crumpled paper bag by his side.

Raya covered her mouth with her hand to muffle a gasp.

He glanced up from his cartoons and eyed her, his gaze traveling efficiently from her bare feet to her styled hair. "You clean up nicely."

"Did you eat my macarons?"

"Were those yours?"

"They were in my hotel room, Phoenix—who did you think they belonged to?" She picked up the crumpled bag. Empty. "You ate all of them? You don't even like eating!"

He shrugged. "They were lumpy, but they tasted pretty good."

Panic rose within her. She didn't even know what the spelled macarons would do to a demon. Sweat prickled on her brow as she slipped her feet into a pair of black ballet flats.

She needed to get out before he developed an urge to share his innermost feelings. "Why don't you just hang out and watch TV? You're welcome to stay." She arranged the leather jacket over her shoulders like a cape.

He made an assenting noise, his attention riveted by the antics onscreen.

Raya slipped out, closing the hotel room door with a quiet click.

14

Raya descended the weathered stone steps to the sidewalk along the left bank of the Seine. The *bateaux* bobbed alongside the pier, their windows shining in the evening sun. The sound of music wafted on the river breeze, punctuated by distant laughter.

She matched the name printed on her ticket to the name of the largest boat at the pier, then presented the ticket to a uniformed attendant. She stepped aboard and felt the deck pitch ever so slightly as the boat rode the gentle waves of the Seine.

A squeal to her left alerted her to the presence of Lizzy.

"You made it!" Lizzy tottered over, wearing four-inch stiletto heels and balancing a full glass of champagne in one hand. Her gold bag swung from her shoulder as she carefully leaned forward to embrace Raya with one arm. "You look amazing."

"Thank you." Raya stepped back to take in Lizzy's hot pink sheath dress and sparkling gold eye makeup. It worked, somehow. "You too."

Lizzy fluttered her free hand. "I've lost Nathan. He's gone off to hide somewhere."

"Do you want me to help you look for him?"

"No, I'm sure he'll turn up. Let's get you some champagne! Have you tried any of these?" She snagged a morsel from a tray of hors d'oeuvres.

Raya selected one for herself and followed in Lizzy's wake as she sailed through the crowd.

When they found a serving table filled with champagne glasses, Lizzy handed one to Raya and took a second glass for herself. The two witches faced a window as the sunset painted the sky a warm shade of pink.

"Are you so excited?" Lizzy didn't wait for an answer. "I am so excited! But also kind of sad." Her lower lip formed a pout as she frowned. "It's over all too fast."

"I can't believe it's already over. Seems like I just got here." Raya sipped from her flute.

"Are you staying, or are you flying home right away?"

"I have a few days extra. I thought I might as well enjoy Paris while I'm here. Who knows when—or if, on my salary—I'll ever get back."

"Of course you'll be back. I'm staying a few days more, too. So is Nathan."

"No kidding?" Raya turned from the window and scanned the crowd. Black was a popular color tonight, liberally garnished with sparkling jewelry. Witches liked to be dramatic in their clothing choices.

"Speak of the devil—there he is!" Lizzy headed toward the back of the boat.

Raya spotted Nathan, clad in his usual tweed jacket with elbow patches, leaning against the rear railing. His conservative attire stood out among the glittering raiment of the rest of the witches.

His expression didn't change as they approached.

"So this is where you've been hiding yourself." Lizzy handed him a glass of champagne.

"I wouldn't call it hiding." He raised the glass and took a small sip. "Hello, Raya."

"Nathan." Raya acknowledged him with a nod and let her gaze travel over the banks of the Seine. Floodlit buildings retreated as the boat rumbled to life and powered through the water.

Lizzy nudged Nathan. "Raya says she's staying a few extra days."

"Really."

She leaned closer to Raya. "Nathan's working on something hush-hush."

Nathan shot Lizzy a look. "Lizzy seems to not understand the 'hush-hush' part."

Lizzy laughed off his remark and sipped her champagne.

Raya blinked. Someone was calling her name. The sound traveled oddly, as if it were coming from the air and bouncing off the water.

Raya looked around the deck. No one else was looking in her direction. She peered into the interior of the boat, where groups of witches mixed, mingled, and danced the night away.

Nothing seemed to be amiss.

"Raya!"

Oh, no. She knew that voice.

A crosswind kicked up, accompanied by the sound of flapping wings.

Outlined in the glow of the city's evening illumination, Phoenix hovered in the air behind the boat.

Horrified, Raya backpedaled from the railing, unable to take her gaze from the demon coming in for a landing.

Lizzy followed Raya's gaze and her mouth fell open in shock.

Nathan's eyes widened as he perceived the demon. He looked from Raya to Phoenix and back again.

Phoenix dove and landed on the deck, facing Raya. His hair blew in the wind as he approached her.

The noise of the party ebbed from the back to the front of the boat as the assembled witches sensed the intruder. A crowd slowly formed as witches drifted closer to the spectacle.

Raya trembled as adrenaline coursed through her. "Phoenix, you have to go." Under normal circumstances, he knew better than to risk being seen by hundreds of witches. God only knew what other effects the magical macarons were having on him.

The demon cast a contemptuous glance over the crowd. "Are you embarrassed of me? In front of your friends?"

Throughout the crowd, clothing rustled as hands fluttered to wands. Some witches stared with frank hostility. Others eyed Phoenix like he was a free sample tray at a gourmet grocery store.

Nathan maintained his position in front of the crowd. "You didn't tell me you had a pet demon."

Phoenix looked Nathan up and down. "Who's this, then? Oh—you're the one who couldn't get enough power on your own, so you got a couple of witches to do the hard work for you."

Nathan's lips quirked with dark amusement.

"He's not my pet!" She stepped closer to Phoenix and spread her arms to shield him from the other witches, who were pressing closer by the second. "Phoenix, get out of here."

He touched her cheek and looked into her eyes as if no one else were present. "But I'm lonely, Raya."

Oh, God. She felt sick. He wasn't in his right mind. She had to make him leave, now, before some enterprising witch decided to banish or bind him right there on the spot. "Phoenix, go away!"

"But—"

"Go, Phoenix!"

Her words landed like blows. He reeled back as if struck, hurt emanating from his eyes. His crimson wings snapped open like a reproof, and he shot into the air, lost to sight in the shifting shadows of the Parisian night.

PHOENIX

15

Phoenix tumbled through the dark sky, riding the downdrafts in a wild freefall only to soar upward at the last moment.

Good thing ordinary Parisians couldn't see him. He was putting on quite the air show.

He surged higher and angled toward a more disreputable neighborhood, leaving the Seine and the boat full of witches behind him. If Raya wouldn't help him, he could at least drown his sorrows at Cosmo's bar.

A tiny voice in the back of his mind told him he wasn't making the best decisions at the moment, but he ignored the voice and plunged ahead.

This time, he didn't need to take the stairs up. He aimed for a window on the second floor and dove through it at full speed, passing through the glass like it was only fog. He skidded to a stop in the middle of the bar as the wind of his landing blasted through the room.

George cradled a fruity drink in both hands and shot him an aggrieved look. "You nearly knocked over my beverage."

"Sorry, mate." Phoenix ran his fingers through his hair and shook his head as if to clear it. "I'm a little off my game."

George carefully set his glass down on the table. "What are you doing here, anyway? I thought you were passing the time with that witch—the one who's not so bad—what's her name?"

"Raya. Apparently, she is that bad. She told me to go away."

George snorted. "What'd you do to her?"

"Do to her? Nothing. I just told her I was lonely." Something sounded wrong about that. Why had he told her he was lonely?

Why in Lucifer's name had he touched her cheek like that?

Cosmo came around the bar and sat next to George at the small round table. "You told someone you were lonely?"

Phoenix rubbed his eyes. "It seemed like the right thing to do. I've never felt so—strongly—about anything."

Cosmo and George looked at each other, then at Phoenix.

"That's not like you," said Cosmo.

George shook his monstrous head, a look of concern on his face.

Phoenix dropped into a chair. "I need a drink."

Cosmo assessed him with a glance. "Maybe the last thing you need is a drink."

"Cosmo, don't be difficult."

She shrugged and went to the bar.

Phoenix rested his head on his arms. "Is this how humans feel all the time?"

George raised an eyebrow like a furry caterpillar. "I wouldn't know."

Cosmo placed a bottle of champagne and a glass in front of Phoenix.

He sat up. "Oh, goody. Little bubbles to make the feelings go away." He filled the glass to the brim and drank it all in one shot.

Cosmo and George exchanged another look.

"Did something happen to you, Phoenix?" Cosmo tried to slide the bottle out of reach.

Phoenix pulled the bottle back and hiccupped. "Nothing happened to me. I watched some cartoons, I ate some macarons, I followed Raya onto a boat full of witches and told her I was lonely."

No, that still didn't sound right at all.

"And some smug little bastard called me Raya's pet demon. Me! A pet." He refilled his glass and slammed the bottle on the table. He tossed the drink back.

Anger felt so much better than loneliness.

George attempted to subtly move the bottle away.

Phoenix glared at him. "Stop it, George. I'm not a child."

George harrumphed. He reached into the pocket of his jacket, which was approximately 200 years out of date, and pulled out a pair of reading glasses. He put them on, leaned closer, and peered at Phoenix.

Phoenix blinked. "You're a demon, George. You don't need glasses."

Unperturbed, George gripped Phoenix's jaw with a clawed hand and examined his face. "You're a demon, Phoenix. You don't need to dress like a GQ model pretending to be a motorcycle hooligan. Are you sure you haven't been hit with a spell lately?"

Phoenix pushed George's hand off and waved the idea away. "I'd know if I had." He abandoned the glass and drank straight from the bottle.

Damn witches.

George removed his glasses and stowed them in the antique jacket. "Cosmo?"

Phoenix attempted to stare Cosmo down while simultaneously drinking from the bottle. It didn't work very well. He managed to dribble champagne down his neck in the process.

Cosmo tilted her head and narrowed her eyes. "Something's affecting you. If not a spell, it's your witch, Raya."

Phoenix righted the bottle and coughed. "She's not my witch. I'm just mad at that stupid mortal, Nathan, for being such an arrogant prat."

"Takes one to know one," said George.

"Shut up, George." He finished the dregs of the champagne. "I know what I'm going to do. I'm going to find that witch, Nathan, and terrorize him to the point where he'll never dare to insult a demon again." Phoenix stood up. Anger bloomed inside him, warming him like a fire. It felt wonderful. "I'll teach him some manners."

Cosmo sprang up and put a hand on his shoulder. "Maybe that isn't such a good—"

Phoenix shook her off and ran for the window. His wings exploded to full length as he dove through it and into the night.

━━━•◦•━━━

Finding Nathan's hotel was child's play. Raya had mentioned it in passing, and Phoenix knew Paris from the inside out.

Now he just had to wait for the witch to fall asleep. Surely he would be exhausted from the party on the boat.

Phoenix perched on the roof, wishing he could talk to his friend Andromalius, currently ensconced with his mortal lover, Erin—in a poky little town in Florida, of all places. He and Andy had viewed Paris as their own, spending many a night raising hell throughout the *arrondissements*.

Instead, he banked his anger to a slow burn and waited, deep in the shadow of a garret, for his chance. He might be flighty, but no one would ever accuse him of not having the patience to wait for the right moment to wreak havoc on someone who had offended him.

The moon crept across the sky. Phoenix remained motionless, a handsome gargoyle of pain and anger, on his rooftop perch—until he sensed Nathan drop into unconsciousness in one of the rooms below.

He smiled to himself. This was going to be fun. Mortals were at their most vulnerable in dreams.

Phoenix descended into Nathan's dreaming mind, appearing in what looked like a shadowy forest. He considered transforming into a hideous monster, but discarded the idea, preferring for Nathan to know exactly who haunted his dreams. He would rue the day he'd ever spoken to Phoenix, and he'd think twice about ever insulting a member of demonkind again.

Through an opening in the trees, Phoenix spotted Nathan.

Nathan stood with his back to Phoenix, seemingly caught up in his own dream, unable to sense the demon silently stalking him.

Phoenix glided noiselessly through the dream woods, preparing to seize control of Nathan's dream and twist it to his own purposes. Should he chase him mercilessly? Or just drag him shrieking into the sky and drop him like a rock, until he awoke drenched in the sweat of his own terror?

So many choices.

He was almost upon Nathan. Oddly, the surroundings seemed more solid than the average mortal's dreamscape. His rage flared again, wiping out any thoughts of hesitation or loneliness or Raya.

Then Nathan turned around and raised one hand.

Phoenix collided with what felt like a brick wall. He recoiled, then struggled as he realized he hadn't just been hit by a brick wall—he'd been surrounded by one.

What was happening? Mortals weren't usually this powerful in dreams. Suddenly, the realistically detailed landscape made sense.

He had unwittingly flown right into a trap.

Nathan calmly regarded his struggles. "Hello, Phoenix."

"What—what did you do to me, you little bastard!" Phoenix twisted and pushed at the invisible restraints.

"Such language."

Phoenix spat a baker's dozen of foul curse words. It didn't help, but it certainly felt better than bowing to Nathan's reproof.

"Such an unpleasant personality, too. And yet Raya keeps you around."

"You keep her name out of your mealy mouth, witch."

Nathan ignored him. "That's the question, isn't it. Why does she keep you around?" He circled Phoenix, examining him from every angle. "You must be valuable."

Phoenix tried to turn his head to follow Nathan's movement but found himself nearly paralyzed.

The walls had closed in.

He rolled his eyes in a show of bravado. At the moment, they were the only thing he could move, other than his mouth. "She doesn't keep me around. I'm not bound to her."

"And yet you sought her out." He leaned into Phoenix's face.

"To tell her you were lonely." His voice rang with contempt. "Maybe you were bound—in a manner of speaking."

"Go to hell."

Nathan's lips twisted into a smile like he knew he'd scored a direct hit. "If you were bound with a spell, she might have noticed if someone stole her pet demon. But now, she'll never know."

"You can't do anything to me in a dream."

Phoenix really hoped Nathan couldn't do anything to him in a dream.

Nathan crossed his arms. "No?"

If Phoenix could have sweat, he would have done so in buckets at the amused look on Nathan's face. He argued the point anyway. "You're asleep. You'll wake up and I'll be gone. Free as a bird."

Nathan's lips quirked. "Really. You don't seem very sure of that."

Phoenix was not at all sure.

"You're only partially correct." Nathan stared at Phoenix like he was deciding which part of a Thanksgiving turkey to carve first. "It's true that I can't bind you to my service in a dream. But I can put you away until I'm ready to make use of you."

"Put me away? You mean banish me?" Banishing wasn't harmful to a demon, but it resulted in disappearing from the mortal world for an unpredictable amount of time. The thought frightened him. No one would know where he had gone.

No one would even know he needed rescuing.

Nathan shook his head and pulled a wand from his pocket. "No, I'm not going to banish you. Too hard to call you back. I'm going to hide you until I'm ready to summon and bind you in the real world."

Phoenix scoffed. "You can't hide a demon."

Nathan leveled the wand at Phoenix.

"Wait! I have powerful friends—if you do this, a legion of demons will come after you and tear your soul to shreds!"

Nathan smirked. "Would these be the demons who have a secret hideout in Paris?"

How the hell did Nathan know about that? "I don't know what you're talking about," he bluffed.

Nathan's eyes glinted. "They're next." With that, he released a wave of power from the dream-wand.

The spell enveloped Phoenix, covering him in a pulsing ultra-violet web that smelled of ancient magic torn from deep within the earth. The magic folded him like an ethereal piece of origami paper. His vision blurred and the ground rushed up at him.

As his sight cleared, he looked up. Why was Nathan so tall? He spat a few more curse words for good measure, but heard only hisses and yowls.

Nathan knelt and hooked a finger into something around Phoenix's neck. He tugged it once, making sure it was secure, then stood up. "*Au revoir.*" Nathan walked into the forest and disappeared.

The forest collapsed into darkness. Phoenix's consciousness shot out of the dream, back to the rooftop and the real world. He balanced himself on four paws to keep from falling off the smooth metal roof.

Paws?

Damn it all.

The witch had turned him into a cat.

16

Phoenix shuddered in an attempt to spread his wings. Nothing happened. He clumsily pawed at the collar around his neck, to no avail. He called for help, but what came out sounded like a yowl and earned only an answering meow from a nearby alley.

He padded on quiet paws to the darkened window of the garret. The moonlit reflection showed his appearance: a diminutive black cat with a snug collar.

Phoenix sat on his haunches on the windowsill.

This was bad.

This was very, very bad.

Also, there was no way he was going to sit around and wait for Nathan to decide he was ready to capture his own pet demon.

Phoenix picked his way across the rooftop and found a rickety fire escape. A series of careful steps and jumps brought him back to the ground. He didn't know if he could be seriously harmed in this form, but he didn't want to find out the hard way.

Despite being unable to feel tired in a physical sense, Phoenix felt overwhelmed by spiritual exhaustion.

If demon cats could sleep, he would have curled up for a catnap right then and there.

But there was no time for that.

Could witches still sense him? Would other demons still recognize him? He paused as he considered his options. Without the ability to fly, navigating Paris would take a lot longer than usual.

He was closer to Cosmo's bar than Raya's hotel.

Decision made, he padded out of the dark alley onto the relatively well-lit sidewalk.

Thanks to the late hour—or early hour, depending on how you looked at it—pedestrians were scarce. No one noticed a small black cat who crept from shadow to shadow.

The street led to a great roundabout where swerving cars dodged each other in a hellish dance around the Arc de Triomphe.

Phoenix retreated from the traffic and darted down a nearby sidestreet. What had been an easy jaunt through the air, just hours before, had turned into miles of slogging on little cat legs.

By the time he got halfway to the bar, there were noticeably more people on the street. He had to be careful to avoid being scooped up by one of the well-meaning early risers.

Now was not the time to get adopted by a sweet little old *grand-mère.*

Trucks rumbled to life in the backstreets as dawn approached. He dodged the deliveries, slipping under parked vehicles and around trundling carts of goods.

In the neighborhood of Cosmo's bar, he had more to worry about from street toughs than *grand-mères.* In normal circumstances, he would have been more than a match for any ten thugs, but without the ability to fly, he didn't want to take any chances.

He found the street-level door. He pressed against it with all of his feline strength but couldn't budge it. He scratched at it with his paws, which did nothing but carve tiny grooves into the wood.

He dashed around the corner to the alley under the bar window just in time to see the first rays of the sun burst across the sky. He watched helplessly as the demons in the bar took to the sky from the window, returning to their own personal haunts and leaving the bar empty until the next night.

No matter how he leaped and yowled, not a single one noticed the tiny kitten down in the alley. Phoenix howled in frustration, too upset to care that it came out as an ungodly caterwaul.

But there was still Raya.

So what if she'd told him to go away. He'd been acting like a maniac, swooping in on her in front of the other witches like that. Surely she'd forgive him. And turn him into himself again.

Phoenix ran as fast as a cat could run.

———◆———

By the time he got to Raya's hotel, the sun beamed down from the high angle of midmorning.

If—no, when—he got his wings back, he'd never set foot on the ground again if he could help it.

He crept closer to the hotel entrance, hoping to intercept Raya on her way out. He settled on his stomach like a Sphinx to watch the door.

Absorbed in his sentry duties, he didn't notice the footsteps behind him until it was too late.

Firm but gentle hands scooped Phoenix from the ground. "*Es-tu perdu?*" He repeated the question in English. "Are you lost?"

Phoenix considered slashing the man's face and running for it, then thought better of it. This man, if he recalled correctly, worked inside the hotel. Perhaps this would be an improvement on watching the door.

Phoenix purred and nuzzled the man's hand.

"You have a collar. Someone must be looking for you."

Phoenix mewled.

"Poor thing! You are all alone in this world." He cradled Phoenix in the crook of his arm and scratched his head.

Phoenix purred some more and hoped no one ever heard about this. Ever.

"Do you want some milk?"

No, he did not. But he would pretend he did if it got him closer to liberation. He extended a tiny, pink cat tongue and delicately licked the man's hand.

He chuckled. "Come on, then." He carried Phoenix into the hotel lobby. "Where can we put you?"

"Ahmed! There you are." Raya ran down the last few stairs and approached the man holding Phoenix. "I was wondering if you could help me."

"Of course. Let me find somewhere to put my new friend for the moment, yes?"

"Do you want me to hold him? I love animals."

Clearly, Raya didn't recognize him.

Phoenix stared at Raya's face, so open and loving in contrast to her usual demeanor with humans. Or demons. This side of her he'd seen only with her dog, Blaze, back at home.

"That would be very helpful. Give me just a moment to get a place set up for him." Ahmed carefully handed him to Raya.

"Oh, isn't he a precious baby." She scratched under his chin and petted his silky head.

This was getting a little out of hand. He meowed in protest.

Raya changed the position in which she was holding him. "Are you a little prince? A little prince who doesn't like his little kitty head scratched?"

Her lilting baby talk was insulting but strangely soothing. It had been a long night. Phoenix gave up protesting and nestled in her arms.

"Attaboy," she murmured, smoothing the fur down his back.

Just as Phoenix got used to lolling in Raya's embrace, Ahmed returned.

"I found a closet for him." He reached for Phoenix.

Raya pulled back. "A closet?"

"Just for now. I put in a little bed, some newspaper. Until we can find his owner. Or a new home."

Phoenix felt Raya's body relax.

"That's all right, then." She transferred Phoenix to Ahmed's arms. "What about tonight, when you're not on shift, though? Will you take him home?"

"My wife—she's allergic." He paused. "Perhaps one of the staff?"

Phoenix reached out a paw toward Raya and meowed pitifully.

"I know! He could stay in my room."

Ahmed looked doubtful. "The management might not like it."

Raya bent level with Phoenix. "But he would. Wouldn't you, my little dark prince?"

Phoenix purred like a sports car.

Ahmed hesitated.

Raya touched the wand in her hair. "I'm sure it will be fine."

That minx. She was spelling the poor man.

Ahmed blinked, then smiled. "You're right. It will be fine. So helpful, really."

Raya gave Phoenix one more caress. "See you tonight, dark prince."

17

Spending the day in a hotel broom closet was no one's idea of fun, but Phoenix endured knowing the end of Ahmed's shift would bring him back to Raya's side.

In cat form, still—but it was better than nothing.

The door to the closet creaked open.

Ahmed poked his head through the doorway. "Kitty cat? Where are you?"

Phoenix stood up, stretched, and meowed, making himself easily seen and heard.

Ahmed scooped him up. "Time to visit your new friend." He scratched between Phoenix's ears.

Phoenix didn't resist. It was actually quite hard to scratch that spot on his own.

Ahmed carried him upstairs along with a few supplies and knocked on Raya's hotel room door. "Madame? It is Ahmed."

The door opened.

Raya let out an uncharacteristic squeal of delight. "My little prince!" She reached for Phoenix.

Ahmed handed him over and set the box of supplies just inside the doorway. "I will call you in the morning when I get here."

Raya nodded, no longer paying much attention to anything but the little black cat she snuggled in her arms. "Thanks, Ahmed." She scooted the box of supplies out of the way with her foot and shut the door. "Aren't we going to have such fun!"

Phoenix nearly lost his focus. It was embarrassingly easy to slip into the role of a pampered cat, especially when it was enhanced by the novel experience of Raya doing the pampering.

He shook his kitty head so hard his ears flapped.

Raya smiled and set him down on the floor. "Aren't you too cute! Look at your funny little ears."

Was there anything he could do that wasn't adorable?

Raya scratched that hard-to-reach spot on his head and cooed.

Apparently not.

He gave up and flopped on the floor like a rag doll. He had to figure out a way to communicate with Raya that didn't involve snuggling. It wasn't getting him any closer to freedom.

Although it was kind of nice, for a change.

Phoenix exiled those addled thoughts to the back of his mind.

He had to focus. He stood up and looked for Raya's wand.

It rested in its usual place in her hair. He had no idea how to get at it, or to encourage her to use it. Perhaps if he could, she would be able to notice that something was amiss.

To do that, he'd have to get closer.

Which meant more snuggling.

How had he gotten back to snuggling so quickly?

Never mind—it was for a good cause.

He padded closer to Raya and bumped her hand with his head. She took the hint. "Do you need another scratch?"

He meowed.

She scratched behind his ears and smoothed the fur over his spine. "I'll tell you what, little prince. Why don't I get changed into some pajamas and we can settle in for some serious cuddling?"

Phoenix purred and tried very hard not to think about how Raya would react when she found out her little prince wasn't actually a cat.

Then she started changing her clothes.

Phoenix flattened himself on the floor, closed his eyes, and attempted to cover them with his paw.

"Aren't you funny! Covering your face like that. You can look now—Mama's dressed."

There could be no doubt, now. She would kill him. Phoenix would have groaned in horror, but his vocal cords didn't work right. What came out sounded like an unholy yowl.

"Oh, come on, these aren't that bad." Raya smoothed out her black pajama tank top and adjusted the waistband of the matching black shorts. "I think they're very nice."

He was beginning to think staying a cat forever might be the safer option.

Raya jumped into bed and patted the covers. "Here, kitty kitty."

Yes, almost definitely the safer option.

He gathered his courage and sprang onto the bed.

Raya reached for the TV remote and flipped channels until she found an action movie—no language skills needed in order to follow the simple plot.

Phoenix settled warily on the pillow next to Raya's head.

Raya burrowed into the covers and relaxed, reaching out occasionally to give him a gentle pat.

He'd never seen her so unguarded.

She would never forgive him.

He tried to relax into the soft pillow while he waited for her to fall asleep. If she fell asleep, he might be able to get her wand. What he would do with it, he didn't know—but it was the only plan he had.

Halfway through the movie, Raya sighed contentedly and switched off the bedside lamp. The glow of the television illuminated the white sheets and threw her features into relief.

After the movie, she turned off the television and rolled on her side, facing Phoenix. "I'm going to turn in, little prince. How about you?" She tickled him under his chin. "You sleepy? Do kitties dream?"

This kitty didn't, but he had no way of telling her that.

She yawned. "Sometimes I have bad dreams. Maybe you can be my little guardian. How about that? You want to guard Mama's dreams?"

Dreams? Maybe there was something to that. He meowed heartily for her benefit.

She settled deeper under the blankets and closed her eyes. "Mmm…goodnight, dark prince."

Phoenix sat quietly and observed her breathing as it became slower and more even. The thought of Nathan suddenly conjuring him away gave an edge of apprehension to his attempt to wait patiently for Raya to fall completely asleep.

He crept toward her, one paw at a time, watching for any sign of wakefulness. He had to be careful not to step on her thick hair, which fanned across the pillow in frizzy waves that smelled of sweetly scented shampoo. He seized the wand in his teeth and tugged it free before backpedaling softly to his pillow.

Now what?

Phoenix set the wand on the pillow and placed a paw on it so it wouldn't roll away. He wasn't sure what, exactly, he had expected to happen. Maybe that he would touch the wand and be instantly transformed.

That hadn't happened.

He concentrated on the wand. Nothing happened. He suppressed the urge to hiss in frustration, for fear it would wake Raya. What else could he try? He couldn't talk, he couldn't fly, he couldn't do anything worthwhile. Unless…

Phoenix took the wand in his teeth and crept to where Raya's hand held the covers loosely. With much maneuvering, he managed to angle the wand just right and slip it under her fingers. He curled into a ball and nestled next to her, maintaining contact with her hand and the wand.

Nathan controlled his physical form and abilities—but perhaps he'd left an unintentional loophole.

Phoenix closed his eyes.

The dream state beckoned just out of reach. It felt like pressing his nose against a glass window. He leaned into the sensation, focusing beyond the barrier to the person within.

He sought the Raya he knew— the brash and combative witch who made a formidable sparring partner—and the Raya whose capacity for love and tenderness revealed itself only to the animals she adored.

Phoenix whispered her name through the barrier that lay between them.

The glass separating him from her dreaming mind splintered and fell away.

In her dream, Raya stood before a fire.

Phoenix crept closer on silent paws.

She was weeping.

He froze. What was this?

She reached toward the fire, as if to rescue something that lay within the flames.

Without thinking, Phoenix ran forward, meowing as loudly as he could manage.

Raya hesitated. "Little prince? What are you doing—never mind." She reached for the fire again, her tears shining in the firelight. "I have to save my books." Her voice broke.

Phoenix placed his body between her and the fire and shook his head slowly, back and forth, in an exaggerated motion. He had to free himself, certainly—but first, he had to stop this dreadful nightmare.

Lost in the logic of the dream, Raya reached over him. "If I don't save them, they'll burn."

Phoenix leaped on her arm and quickly climbed up to her shoulder.

Her eyes widened with surprise. As her attention shifted, the fire disappeared.

Then the walls of the dream lit up with thousands of pieces of stained glass.

Raya approached the glowing panes in a daze, with Phoenix riding on her shoulder. As her fingers grazed the surface, the panes rearranged themselves in different patterns, forming intricate geometric shapes under her touch.

From his perch on Raya's shoulder, Phoenix trailed a paw on the glass and found that he could have the same effect. He concentrated. The stained glass under his paw rearranged itself until it formed a perfectly rendered portrait of a small black cat.

Raya smiled. "It's you!"

Phoenix patted the glass with his paw again. This time, the panes rearranged to form a red demon, complete with horns and a tail—and what looked like a black leather jacket.

18

Raya stared at the stained glass. The multicolored light reflected in her eyes. "I've seen this before."

Phoenix reached out a paw and changed the image again.

Cat.

Demon.

Cat.

Raya's brow furrowed. Her lips parted as if she were about to speak.

The dream trembled. The glass walls shook, then collapsed in a roar of breakage that sent Phoenix hurtling out of the dream.

He opened his eyes in the darkness of the hotel room.

Raya gasped and sat up, accidentally knocking Phoenix sideways. "Oh! I'm sorry!" She put her hand to her temple and realized her wand was in her hand. She lowered the wand and stared at it. "How did I end up holding—" Her expression reflected confusion followed by dawning recall. She looked at the cat in her bed and narrowed her eyes. "You were in my dream."

Phoenix righted himself and sat on his haunches, then batted his collar with one paw.

Raya picked him up and examined the collar. "This doesn't even have a buckle. How did you get this on in the first place?" She placed him back on the bed and toyed with her wand thoughtfully.

Phoenix swiped at the wand with his paw before swiping at his own collar again.

Raya tilted her head. "The wand? Your collar?"

He meowed.

"You're a strange one, little dark prince." Raya swung her legs off the bed and stood up. "Since you're not letting me sleep, let's have a closer look at you." She picked him up and carried him to the table, then sat down in the chair. She wrapped one hand around his feline shoulders, steadying his body as she brought the wand close with her other hand.

Phoenix felt rather than saw the moment when she pushed a delicate strand of magic through the wand and into the collar.

The collar began to glow.

Raya braced him more firmly and closed her eyes.

The force of her grip slid his body toward her. He felt her power envelop him, flooding through the seemingly infinite chains binding him to the form of a cat.

One link in the chain snapped. Then another. Then on and on, each and every magical link snapping in a dizzying cascade of tiny sparks until the form that held him unfolded, freeing him at last.

Phoenix found himself crouched on all fours on the table, which wobbled and fell over before he had time to balance himself on it. His wings shot out to full length and he caught himself before he hit the floor, landing neatly on two feet—instead of four.

Raya jumped out of the chair and out of the way. "Phoenix? What the hell is going on? What did you do with the cat?"

"I was the cat!"

Raya covered her mouth as she gasped. "You pretended to be a cat?"

"No, I didn't pretend to be a cat! Your lovely friend Nathan decided to put me on ice until he could trap me for good."

Raya sank into the chair. "Nathan?"

"Yes, Nathan—the one who called me your pet demon, remember? Turns out he's not actually opposed to the idea. He just wants one for himself." Phoenix smoothed his hands over his body, making sure nothing was amiss.

She crossed her arms. "So you found a way to sneak into my hotel room?"

"I wasn't trying to—bloody hell, woman! I was trapped! As a cat! What did you expect me to do?"

"Not sneak into my hotel room, for a start!"

"Nathan caught me in his dreams and turned me into a stupid, helpless, ridiculous cat! I couldn't get to Cosmo's, so I came here."

Surely that would mollify her.

"Wait a minute." Raya held her hand up. "I pet that cat. I snuggled that cat. And all that time—" Her mouth dropped open. She looked down at herself as if just realizing she was wearing pajamas. "Oh, my God." She stood abruptly, crossed the space to the bathroom, went inside, and shut the door.

It had not mollified her at all. Phoenix righted the fallen table, then tread carefully to the bathroom and tapped softly on the door. "Raya?"

No answer.

"Raya, I'm sorry."

The door flung open.

"You're sorry?" She stared at him skeptically, still haughty even in her pajama set. She ticked off his offenses on her fingers. "You snuck into my room, watched me change clothes—"

"Hey! I did not! I covered my eyes. You noticed—you even said it was cute! Remember?"

Raya continued like he hadn't spoken. "I tucked you in and patted you like some kind of blithering idiot, and then, to top it all off, you snuck into my dreams! My dreams, Phoenix!"

"I'm sorry! I didn't know what else to do." He backed away to give her space. "You never told me you had nightmares."

She turned away and leaned on the sink. "You never asked."

"Was that—real? Did someone burn your things? Were those your witchcraft books?"

Raya sighed and hung her head. "My family. It was a long time ago."

"Your family?" Phoenix dredged his memory for the sparse details she'd shared about her family. "I thought you said your family wasn't particularly religious."

"I lied, okay? I didn't want anybody asking me about it. It's not exactly my favorite subject."

"How am I supposed to understand you if you never tell me anything?" He raked his fingers through his hair in frustration before changing tack. "I'm sorry that happened to you. Would you like me to visit their dreams and throw them off a cliff repeatedly?"

That made her laugh. It was a rueful laugh, but a laugh all the same.

"You've gotten into enough trouble sneaking into people's dreams, I think." She emerged from the bathroom and sat on the edge of the bed. "So Nathan trapped you in a dream?"

"Apparently, in addition to being an awful prat, he's very good at lucid dreaming. He caught me and transformed me in the dream, and it stuck."

Raya twisted up her hair and stuck her wand into the bun. "What were you doing in his dreams, anyway?"

He shrugged. "He was rude to me. I wanted revenge. That's what demons do."

"What does he want with you?"

"I think he wants a pet demon. Maybe a lot of pet demons. He seems to know that we have a hangout in Paris."

They looked at each other.

"You better warn Cosmo," she said.

"I know." Looking at Raya made him feel funny. He looked away and stared at the floor. "I saw her and George after the party. I was so angry. They tried to stop me from going after Nathan, but I didn't listen." He rubbed his forehead. "I don't know what I was thinking."

Raya cleared her throat. "I think I might be able to explain." A blush crept over her cheeks. "Those macarons you ate?"

Phoenix raised his eyebrows, waiting for her to continue.

"They were spelled."

"You spelled me?"

She smacked her hands on the bedding. "Not on purpose! You weren't supposed to eat them!"

"You don't think you could have mentioned, 'Oh, by the way, Phoenix, those macarons will make you embarrass yourself'?"

"I didn't know!"

"Like hell you didn't. You made them! Then you snuck out to the party, expecting me to sit here and watch cartoons like a fool until it wore off?"

Raya looked down and didn't answer.

"And then—absolutely not in my right mind—I fly after you onto a boat full of witches who look at me like I'm either a menace or a snack, and then I blather nonsense in front of the whole crowd!"

Her head snapped up. "What do you mean, 'nonsense'? You're going to tell me you're not lonely?"

He tried to sputter a retort, but couldn't get it out before she interrupted.

"Those macarons don't make you lose your mind, Phoenix. They just make your feelings come to the surface."

"Well, you eat them, then—and then you can tell me all about your sadness over people burning your stuff!"

They glared at each other.

It was the worst possible time to remember how much he'd liked it when she called him her dark prince.

19

Phoenix folded his wings away completely and went to the window. If he had to make eye contact for one more second, he'd go mad. Better to pretend to look out at the night.

Raya shifted on the bed. "You should go. You can't be comfortable hanging around a witch, anyway, since you think we're all power-mad, demon-trapping lunatics."

He laughed. "I'm sorry—you're not? I didn't get that memo." He rounded on her. "I wouldn't dream of imposing on someone who thinks demons are just a bunch of flighty, unreliable, pleasure-seeking dilettantes."

Raya marched over and pointed her finger at him. "I don't think demons are a bunch of flighty, unreliable, pleasure-seeking dilettantes. I think *you're* a flighty, unreliable, pleasure-seeking dilettante."

He stood taller, looming over her. "Is that so? Well, you're—" He stopped. It took a herculean effort to check himself before he said something stupid. He closed his eyes and concentrated, then opened them again. "*You're* the only person who can help me stop Nathan."

From the expression on her face, he might as well have hit her in the back of the head with a cartoon frying pan. "You're not going to say something—rude?"

He shook his head, not trusting himself to speak.

She raised an eyebrow.

"I need your help, all right? Warning Cosmo and George and the others isn't enough. If Nathan's looking for all of us, none of us are safe until he's neutralized."

Raya considered. "This is novel—you asking me for help."

"Don't rub it in, witch."

"Wouldn't dream of it, demon. Or should I say, 'my little dark prince'?" Raya ruffled his hair and darted away, giggling.

"Don't you dare call me little."

"Oh, I'm scared now!" She fell over on the bed, laughing uncontrollably.

"Some help you are."

Raya sat up and wiped tears from her eyes. "I'll be serious." She crossed her legs and folded her hands primly. "Just the facts, ma'am."

"That's better."

"Also, I'm hungry."

Phoenix covered his face with his hands. If he were able to die, this woman would be the death of him. "Now you're hungry?"

"Hey, a girl's gotta eat. I didn't even get a full night's sleep, thanks to your dream shenanigans."

"Shall I go? Shall we let Nathan enslave an unlimited amount of demons just because you need a nap and a cookie?"

"Don't be a pill. Just because you don't need food or sleep, doesn't mean we poor mortals can do the same." She threw a pillow at him. "And I don't need a cookie. I need a meal. So shut up and let's move."

"Is that what you're wearing?"

"Why? Would you be embarrassed?" She shimmied her shoulders at him.

If he showed any hint of embarrassment, she'd wear her pajamas in the streets of Paris just to get his goat. He schooled his expression to neutral. "Of course not. The lady wears what the lady chooses," he added diplomatically.

"Well, since you put it so nicely, this 'lady' is going to go change. Privately. In the bathroom." She retreated, but peeked around the doorframe for one last shot. "Away from the prying eyes of naughty little kitties."

"Don't call me a—" he started, but she laughed merrily and slammed the bathroom door before he could finish.

Outside, Phoenix glanced at the sky for a hint of how soon the sun would rise. It looked like they would have just enough time to make it to Cosmo's before the demons abandoned the night's recreation.

At a nearby Métro station, they hopped on the first train of the day, populated by a handful of early morning Parisians.

When they arrived at their station, Raya stopped him. "Aren't you going to blindfold me?"

"What for? Are you going to go running off to Nathan to tell him where the demons hang out?"

"No. But being blindfolded was kind of fun."

"You have a weird idea of fun."

"And you don't, Mr. Dream-Crasher?"

At least she wasn't calling him her little dark prince. "Fine, we have equally weird ideas of fun."

Raya made a satisfied noise.

With the neon lights off and the streets virtually deserted, the neighborhood looked more lonely than seedy. He wished he could have shown Raya the place in its heyday, full of artists and composers mingling in the cafes and cabarets.

They took the stairs to the door of Cosmo's bar.

Phoenix paused. "This time, maybe let me do the talking?"

"I'll say what I like, thank you very much."

Managing Raya was like herding a cat. He should know—he'd been one. Phoenix opened the door.

Demons at the bar and tables scarcely glanced up before returning to their own conversations, recognizing Raya and deeming her harmless—thanks to Cosmo's endorsement.

How little they knew.

From his usual table, George raised his usual fruity beverage.

Phoenix nodded to him and addressed Cosmo at the bar. "Cosmo, set us up, please. And grab one for yourself. We need to talk."

Raya elbowed him in the side. "Aren't you masterful."

They slid into chairs at George's table.

George leaned in. "Back so soon? Did you give that mortal what for?"

"Not exactly."

Raya snorted.

Cosmo set down a tray of drinks and took the fourth chair. "What's this all about, Phoenix?"

Phoenix picked up a drink. "Now, stay calm—"

Cosmo rolled her eyes. "That's exactly what you shouldn't say if you want someone to stay calm."

"And for Lucifer's sake, don't interrupt."

Cosmo mimed zipping her lips and throwing away the key.

Phoenix took a drink before continuing. "We have a problem. The witch that Raya went out in the woods with—"

"Nathan," said Raya.

"Yes, thank you. Are you telling this story, or shall I?"

Raya batted her eyelashes innocently. "Go ahead."

George chuckled.

"Nathan is trying to capture demons."

Cosmo shrugged. "What's new? That's what witches do. That's why I don't let any in here that aren't vetted." She nodded to Raya.

"You don't understand," Raya said. "He doesn't want to capture a demon. He wants to capture all the demons. At least, all the demons in Paris."

Cosmo laughed. "That's not possible. No witch is that powerful."

Phoenix shot Raya a look. "Tell her."

Raya sighed. "Not normally, no. But Nathan found a source of power too big to draw from on his own, and—"

Cosmo raised a delicate eyebrow. "And?"

Raya looked down at the table. "And…I helped him draw from it."

"You what?" Cosmo's raised voice attracted the attention of the demons at a nearby table.

"I didn't know what he was planning to do!"

"You didn't think to ask?"

Phoenix looked back and forth between the woman and the woman-shaped demon, ready to dive under the table if things got dicey.

Raya swirled the liquid in her glass. "I didn't think it was my business, any more than it was his business to ask me what I planned to do with my share." She glanced at Phoenix. "I'm sorry. I was in over my head, and I was blind to the consequences."

Raya had admitted she did something wrong. Phoenix could have been knocked over with a feather.

George tapped the table and snapped Phoenix out of his temporary trance. "How did you find out what he was planning? Does this have something to do with why you ended up here in a tizzy the other night?"

"The other way around, really. I only found out because I ended up here 'in a tizzy,' as you say. I went after Nathan in his sleep, thinking I could have a bit of fun, you know—"

George and Cosmo nodded knowingly.

"Thinking he was the typical helpless mortal in his dreams, but"—Phoenix winced—"he wasn't."

Cosmo's eyes got wide. "What did he do?"

"He turned him into a cat," said Raya.

George leaned back, thunderstruck. "No!"

"And it stuck?" said Cosmo.

Phoenix nodded. "It stuck. He wanted to bind me outright, but it wouldn't work in the dream, and he didn't want me to escape, so he transformed me and stuck some sort of witchy tracking collar on me." He rubbed his neck and shuddered at the memory.

Cosmo set down her glass. "Why didn't you go for help?"

"I couldn't fly, I couldn't talk, I couldn't do anything. I came here straightaway but couldn't even get past the front door. So I went to her." He tilted his glass toward Raya.

Cosmo looked at Raya with obvious respect. "You figured it out and freed him?"

Raya's color, always easy to bring out, flushed her cheekbones instantly. She drank from her glass and nodded rather than respond verbally.

He assumed she was thinking of the pajamas and the snuggling and the "little dark prince" endearments. Time to move on before anyone got interested in the details. "Anyway, we think Nathan has a bead on this place. I think you all need to scatter for a while, at least until we figure this out."

George wrapped his clawed hands protectively around his drink. "I don't want to scatter. I want to stay here and drink with my friends."

"I'm not running from some power-mad witch." Cosmo cracked her knuckles loudly.

Several demons glanced up at the sound and scooted their chairs farther away.

20

When Cosmo cracked her knuckles, any demon with sense stayed out of her way. Phoenix didn't have the luxury of backing down. "Not running, Cosmo. Outsmarting."

"Don't patronize me, Phoenix. We've been here for hundreds of years." She placed her hand on the table in a proprietorial gesture. "Do you think I'm going to pull up stakes and run at the first sign of trouble?"

"Again—not running. This witch has to be brought under control." He glanced at Raya. "We can't do that if we're worrying about protecting this place simultaneously. Be reasonable. Please."

Cosmo downed the last of her drink. "What do you think, George?"

George polished his reading glasses thoughtfully before addressing Phoenix. "How do you know you can handle him? He seemed to get the better of you at your last meeting."

"I don't know that I can handle him. That's where Raya comes in—and possibly a few other allies."

Cosmo eyed him skeptically. "Since when do you have allies?"

"I have plenty of allies, thank you very much."

"Name one."

"I happen to know a powerful angel who would be very interested to know about a witch exceeding his limits."

George made a quizzical face. "Isn't that the angel who threatened to decapitate you with a flaming sword if he ever saw your face again?"

Raya sat forward in her chair. "Hold up—angels are real?"

All three demons looked at her with amusement.

George spoke first. "It's not commonly known. They're in hiding, mostly. Too much pressure."

"Pressure from what?"

George shrugged his massive shoulders. "Keeping the peace. Being customer service representatives for a deity. It's a hard job."

Phoenix leaned back and laced his fingers behind his head with a grin. "One benefit of being a demon: low expectations."

Raya shot him a look. "Don't I know it."

"You really think this is serious enough to call in outside help?" asked Cosmo.

Phoenix nodded.

"Fine. I'll go along—for now. Use the Dead Drop to keep us informed. If we're going to go to the trouble of staying away from each other, we might as well take it seriously."

Raya looked confused. "What's a dead drop? Like for spies?"

Phoenix stood up before replying to Cosmo. "Meanwhile, I need to get this mortal some food and sleep."

"Mortals," said George, shaking his head.

"Hey, now—don't talk about me like I'm not here!" Raya stifled a yawn.

"It's all right, darling. We only tease the ones we love." Cosmo winked at Raya. "Isn't that right, Phoenix?"

Thoroughly flustered and willing to do almost anything to end the conversation, Phoenix pretended he hadn't heard. "We're off, then."

"Sleep tight," said George. "Metaphorically speaking, of course, Phoenix."

Phoenix and Raya took the stairs and exited into the fresh, clear sunlight of the early morning.

Raya looked around. "So, where's breakfast?"

"At a restaurant, I presume?"

"No, I mean where can you find a real breakfast—eggs, bacon, orange juice—the works?"

"That's an American thing. The French get by on coffee, cigarettes, and the occasional croissant."

"*Vive la France* and all, but I want a damn omelet. If you're such an expert on Paris..."

Of course she would sting his vanity to get him to do what she wanted. "Challenge accepted."

He ushered her to a nearby cafe, white and bright in its decor in contrast to the old-school brasserie at which he'd stolen her fries.

They slid into spindle back chairs made of honey-colored wood.

Raya took one look at the menu and slid it across the burnished grain of the table. "Do your magic."

"Don't you want to know what's on it?"

"Surprise me."

Phoenix ordered a little of everything. No harm in giving her choices.

When the waiter delivered her orange juice, Raya wrapped her hands around the glass and drank in a way that made her seem younger than she really was. It was her air of enthusiasm, even over the smallest things, that gave the impression.

Phoenix gestured toward the large windows facing the street. "So why haven't you partnered up with one of those mortals running around out there?"

Raya slammed the glass down and started coughing. "What?"

"You heard me."

She cleared her throat. "I haven't 'partnered up' because I haven't met anyone I want to partner up with."

"You're young, you're attractive, you're successful. I don't see the difficulty."

Raya looked at him like he had two heads. "Everyone is young to you, Phoenix."

"Given."

"Why do you ask?"

"Just curious." He stared out the window at the people passing by.

"How about you? Has there ever been a special demon in your life?"

"I've known the lot of them for so long that most of them are like siblings now."

Raya carefully took a sip of her juice. "Mortals, then?"

He shrugged eloquently. "Nothing serious."

She snickered. "Could've predicted that."

"Oh, do I amuse you? Doesn't sound like you've ever been that serious with anyone, either, witch."

"Be quiet, little prince, before I spoil your perfect hair with this orange juice."

It took two waiters to deliver the food, piled high on an assortment of sturdy white stoneware plates.

Raya's eyes widened. "Is this all for me? There's no way I can eat this much."

"I didn't know what you wanted. So I ordered everything."

She pointed to a bowl. "What's this?"

"That's *shakshuka*. Baked eggs with peppers and spices. And these are orange water pancakes with ricotta, and that's a full English breakfast. Baked beans, mushrooms, fried eggs. And I believe this is a brioche bun stuffed with bacon, eggs, and spinach."

"Holy cow."

"I think that's the only thing I didn't order."

Raya dived in, sampling from all the plates. "Come on, you have to try this," she said around a mouthful of pancakes. "Don't give me that garbage about how you don't eat. I already know you're a liar and a french fry stealer."

"You promise you haven't put a spell on this?"

"Ha, ha. Very funny. Now shut up and get in here."

That first stolen fry had forced him to admit he could be made to feel from something so fleeting as food. Now, faced with a breakfast of epic proportions, he found himself wanting to revel in the sensations of the moment, all thoughts of witches or demonkind suspended in favor of just enjoying a plate of eggs and present company.

He picked up the bun, made eye contact with Raya, and bit into it.

A smile played across her lips.

Together, they demolished the meal.

When they were finished, Raya staggered onto the sidewalk, groaning theatrically and holding her middle. "Remind me never to try to keep up with a supernatural being when it comes to competitive eating."

Phoenix steered her in the direction of the nearest Métro station. "Methinks it's time for your nap."

She actually nodded off on the train, its soothing motion lulling her until her head drooped on his shoulder.

He debated whether to wake her.

It was only a fifteen minute ride.

He gently positioned her head and let her sleep.

When they arrived at her station, he woke her. "We're here."

They walked the short distance to her hotel as the streets filled with the usual morning traffic.

As they entered the lobby, Ahmed hailed Raya from the front desk. "I was going to call you, madame. How is our little guest?"

Raya shot a mischievous glance at Phoenix. "He was just lovely. Very well-behaved. I'd take care of him anytime."

"Shall I take him off your hands?"

Raya's mouth opened and closed. She clearly hadn't thought that far, and the heavy breakfast and lack of sleep seemed to inhibit her ability to lie on the fly.

Phoenix intervened. "We ran into the owner outside the hotel early this morning. He was very relieved."

"So relieved," added Raya.

Ahmed's gaze traveled between Phoenix and Raya. "Oh? Well, I guess all is well that ends well."

Raya nodded enthusiastically and darted up the stairs before he could ask any more questions.

Phoenix gave the clerk a little salute and followed Raya to her room.

Inside, she flopped on the bed like a starfish. "I could sleep for a week."

"Not for a week. We have a rogue witch to stop, remember?"

She sighed and covered her face with a pillow. "Fine." The word came out very muffled.

He snatched the pillow away. "Shall I come back in a few hours?"

She looked up at him. "Come back? Where are you going?"

"I don't know. Anywhere, I guess."

She rolled over to the nightstand, picked up the television remote, and held it out to him. "Here. You don't have to go. You can watch TV, if you want. I'll sleep right through it."

For the first time in a long time, uncertainty crept through him. He hesitated, then took the remote.

Their fingers brushed.

"Thanks." He eased into a chair as if sudden movement might startle her into changing her mind.

She stood up and stretched. "You don't mind if I change, do you? It's nothing you haven't already seen, anyway."

The black pajama set? "Of course not. Go right ahead."

Raya scooped up the set from a dresser drawer and retreated to the bathroom.

Phoenix fixed his gaze on the television's mindless drivel and tried very hard to think about anything but a headstrong witch in black pajamas.

21

Raya opened her eyes, stretched, and sat up in bed. She squinted at the TV. "What on earth are you watching?"

"*Le Juste Prix*. Get dressed. We're going to a bakery."

"But I'm still full!"

"We're not going for the food. We're going to talk to the baker."

Raya tossed pillows out of the way as she clambered out of the bed. "Did it ever occur to you to try making sense when you talk?"

"What's the point? You'd only ask silly questions." He dodged the pillow she flung at his head.

Phoenix turned off the French version of "The Price Is Right" and waited for her to dress. If she didn't like his cryptic answer, she really wasn't going to like his straightforward one.

Raya emerged from the bathroom, fully dressed but still rubbing the sleep from her eyes. "All right, Captain Mysterious, where are we really going?"

"I told you."

"A bakery?"

"Right down the street."

"You're joking."

"I am not." Phoenix stood up. Better to have this conversation out in the open, where she'd be less likely to yell at him.

Who was he kidding? Nothing was going to make that less likely.

He stopped her on the sidewalk just outside the hotel. "Do you remember why you chose this hotel?"

She shrugged. "Someone said it was in a nice neighborhood near the convention center?"

"Right. That someone was me, remember?"

"So?" Raya shaded her eyes from the sun and watched the traffic go by.

"So, I may not have been completely straightforward about that."

She rounded on him. "What do you mean, 'not completely straightforward'?"

"I mean, I may have omitted a small amount of information about this particular location."

Raya looked up and down the street as if she expected a parade of demons to start at any moment. "What exactly is in this neighborhood, Phoenix?"

"A friend. Sort of."

Her eyes narrowed. "What friend—"

"I wanted someone around to make sure you were safe if I wasn't here."

"You had someone spying on me?" Her voice increased in volume.

Phoenix winced. "No, not spying! Watching for any unusual magic. These gatherings attract all sorts—as you well know."

"I think I can handle myself, Phoenix. After all, aren't you the one in need of help right now? Maybe your friend should have been babysitting you, instead."

"Look, you can beat me with a stick later, if you like. But for now, can we go talk to her?"

"Don't think I'll forget."

"I know you won't. I'll even find you a stick."

At the entrance to the neighborhood bakery, Phoenix held the door open and allowed Raya to precede him.

The baker had her back to them as they entered, her short, sand-colored hair just visible under her baker's cap.

Phoenix cleared his throat. "Bonjour, madame."

She stiffened, then turned slowly to face them. "You weren't supposed to come here," she said evenly. Her long fingers casually wrapped around a nearby rolling pin. "You have one chance to explain."

Raya stared. "I thought you said you had a friend on this street…"

The baker's gaze shifted from Phoenix to Raya. "This wasn't part of the deal."

Phoenix raised his hands in a placating gesture. "I know, Justine. I know. But things have changed."

Justine shifted the position of the rolling pin. "I did what you asked."

This was not going well.

"You did—and I'm grateful—"

"I owed you a favor. I paid it. We were, as you put it, square." Justine's white clothing began to glow, highlighting her features with an otherworldly light. "And now you enter my place of business, a place from which you are forbidden, and you want to 'talk'?"

This was really not going well.

A look of dawning comprehension passed over Raya's face. "You're not a baker—you're an angel!"

Justine's lips quirked in a sad half-smile. "To my eternal regret."

Raya bounced up and down. "A real angel! This is awesome! Phoenix, you didn't tell me there was an angel right here!"

"No one is supposed to know I'm here, child. I'm retired."

"Really?" Raya leaned on the counter, fascinated. "But you were doing a favor for Phoenix?"

Justine shot Phoenix a look of un-angelic annoyance. "Unfortunately."

Raya gestured to Phoenix with a casual thumb. "I could always tell he was a demon, but I couldn't tell anything about you until you started to glow."

Justine acknowledged Raya's words with a slight nod. "One of the differences between angels and demons."

"Wait a minute—what was all that charade about not speaking English when I came into the shop before?"

Justine lowered the rolling pin and smiled sheepishly. "I didn't think you'd expect a French baker to speak English."

"I'll forgive you if you'll let me try one of these." Raya pointed to one of the more decadent-looking pastries in the case.

"That's a *religieuse*. A nun. Double-decker choux pastry filled with vanilla cream and topped with dark chocolate." Professional pride seemed to be taking the edge from Justine's voice, and the glow that had surrounded her faded out.

Raya's eyes shone. "That's incredible. A nun-baking angel. I bet you could tell some stories."

Was Justine actually blushing?

"One or two."

Phoenix wondered if he should speak at all, or just leave the softening up to Raya. She really was quite good at it.

"Was Phoenix always this insufferable?"

Justine let out a laugh like she and Raya were old friends. "Always. He might even have been worse in the old days."

"Hey, now—"

"In fact"—Justine leaned toward Raya confidentially— "my brother, Justinian, once threatened to cut off his head with a flaming sword."

Raya gasped in mock horror. "No!"

Justine nodded.

Raya shot Phoenix an amused look. "I've felt the same way many times."

Phoenix rolled his eyes. "Great. Now that we all have 'hating Phoenix' in common, could we perhaps get down to business?"

"Shut up, demon," said Justine.

Raya cracked up.

Phoenix threw his hands in the air. "Laugh it up, witch."

Justine caught Raya's mirth and began giggling.

Trust Raya to corrupt even an angel. "I'm glad I amuse the two of you. Meanwhile, there's a witch out there trying to capture every demon in Paris. Would either of you like to do something about it?"

Justine sobered. "I'm sorry, Phoenix, but I've spent too long out of the game to get involved now. I've created a life for myself here."

"I don't want you to get involved. I want you to put me in touch with your brother."

Raya's mouth fell open. "The angel who threatened to remove your head?"

Justine sighed and leaned against the counter. "My brother is in hiding, Phoenix. He's been in hiding for hundreds of years now. Not to mention the fact that you are quite possibly the very last being on earth Justinian would want to see."

A line appeared between Raya's eyebrows. "Your brother's name is Justinian? And, also, since when do angels have siblings?"

"Sometimes it just ends up that way." Justine picked up two *religieuses* and placed them on the display case about a foot apart. "You spend enough time together, you work for a common cause, you become like family." She slid the two pastries together.

"But your names—"

"Are like our forms. They're what we choose." She slid one of the pastries in Raya's direction.

Raya picked up the *religieuse*, took a bite, and chewed thoughtfully. "Phoenix said something like that at Cosmo's. Or was it at breakfast?"

Interest flashed across Justine's face. "Cosmo's?"

Raya set the pastry down. "Have you been there?"

Justine stammered slightly. "No. I mean, I know Cosmo—but I haven't seen her in centuries."

"Literally," said Phoenix.

"She was a terrible thief. Used to sneak in at night and take as many pastries as she could carry." Justine sounded almost wistful. "After a while I would just leave her favorites out on a tray."

Phoenix had no idea how to respond to that tidbit of information.

"That's so sweet," Raya said. "Why don't you go see her?"

"I promised myself I'd stay away." The wrinkles around Justine's eyes deepened as she frowned.

Raya spoke softly. "She's in danger, Justine. They all are. They need help."

Justine's form wavered for a fraction of a second, revealing impossibly creamy white wings shot through with gold, and a corona that outlined her head with a blaze of glory. The vision disappeared as quickly as it had come. "Justinian is hiding underground. I leave him treats, sometimes, near a hidden entrance to the tunnels."

"Take us there, and we won't just be square, Justine—I'll owe you whatever you want."

Justine eyed him. "Whatever I want?"

"Cross my heart." He gestured to match the words.

"You don't have a heart, Phoenix."

He shrugged. "Metaphorically speaking."

22

Phoenix sent Raya back to the hotel, insisting that she rest and recuperate before their evening rendezvous with Justine, who would meet them after the bakery closed.

Raya, predictably, argued like a debate team president, but was eventually cozened into complying thanks to lavish promises of adventure, magic, and angelic encounters to come.

Meanwhile, he had business to conduct.

Invisible to all but other supernatural beings and witches, and unencumbered by a mortal companion, he spread his wings and took to the air, hovering over the 7th *arrondissement* with its elegant old buildings before angling across the Seine.

Notre Dame stood sentry over the Île de la Cité in the middle of the river. He dove between its two largest towers just for fun, watching the tourists mill about in the plaza below. He considered making himself visible and swooping down for a startling fly-by, but decided that he'd angered enough angels in the vicinity of the cathedral and probably shouldn't court trouble if he planned on asking one for help.

Past the Seine and a few dozen streets over, he landed at the gates to a vast cemetery. The cobblestone paths wound under tall trees that cast shifting shadows on the graves and vaults below.

Phoenix had known more than a few of the permanent residents.

Allowing himself a single sigh for centuries gone by, he ghosted through the crowd at the entrance and continued deeper into the necropolis, past statues of shrouded, weeping mourners.

Stone angels with stained wings kept a blank-eyed watch as he veered off the path into a tangled jumble of neglected gravesites.

He stopped before a vault, wider and taller than the rest, with a flattened roof fully exposed to the sky above due to a lack of trees in the immediate area. A quick pulse of his wings allowed him to land lightly on top.

The Dead Drop had been used in years past to leave messages in times of upheaval—and in peaceful times, the more mischievous demons had left behind a motley collection of rude words, bad puns, and the occasional drawing in questionable taste. The Dead Drop functioned something like a whiteboard in a break room, requiring only a quick flight over the cemetery to reveal the inscriptions left by other demons.

Phoenix bent to the task, tracing his finger over the stone roof of the vault. "Rogue witch exceeding his powers," he muttered as he inscribed the words. "Do not congregate. Do not make yourself known. Remain hidden until I give the all-clear. By the authority of Phoenix, Great Marquis of Hell. That should do it." He straightened and dusted his hands. "No, wait." He bent low again. "P.S.—Cosmo: Justine says hi."

A rustling sound in the distance, different from the sounds of the tree branches in the breeze, made him turn instinctively. "Come out, whoever you are. I can hear you."

Cosmo's cobalt wings extended above the stone angel she was hiding behind. Her head peeked out from behind the statue's head. "I heard my name."

"Speak of the devil." Phoenix sat on the edge of the vault's roof, letting his legs dangle over the side.

Cosmo alighted and sat next to him, then leaned back and studied what he had written. "Justine mentioned me?" she said casually.

Almost too casually.

"Something about stolen pastries."

Cosmo grinned.

"By the way, Cosmo, the whole point of the Dead Drop is to avoid meeting up, remember? What are you doing lurking around the necropolis?"

"Looking for news."

"You could have looked from the air."

"You only follow the rules when it suits you, Phoenix—why should I be any different?" She tucked her hair behind her ears. "For such a rebel as you claim to be, you're quite stuffy."

"I am not!"

"Are too. You can't even bring yourself to admit why you're hanging around that witch all the time. Some rebel you are."

Phoenix mustered as much haughty dignity as he could manage. "I hang around Raya because she's amusing—for a mortal."

Cosmo laughed. "I knew demons were good at lying, but I never knew any as good as you at lying to themselves."

"It's none of your business, anyway."

"See? Stuffy. I told you so."

"Oh, go steal a pastry." Phoenix crossed his arms.

"Not until I get the real news—not this memo to the masses." She gestured over her shoulder at the writing on the roof.

"I talked to Justine."

"And?"

"She doesn't want to get involved—"

A crooked smile touched Cosmo's lips. "Sounds like Justine."

"But she agreed to take us to where her brother is hiding out."

Cosmo looked at him, eyes wide. "He of the flaming sword?"

"The very same." Phoenix made a motion like swinging a sword horizontally through the air.

"Good luck. You'll need it." Cosmo jumped down with agile grace, her blue wings slowing her fall, then looked up at Phoenix when she landed. "When you see Justine—tell her…I haven't found another bakery I like as much."

Phoenix made a face. "I'm not telling her that."

Cosmo showed her teeth when she smiled. "You will or I'll break your face."

"All right, calm down, you mad thing. I'll pass along your message."

She darted away and disappeared from sight.

Phoenix watched the dead leaves spiral down from the wind-tossed trees before picking up a slender green branch to bring back to Raya.

23

He knocked on Raya's hotel room door, then held up the branch as she opened it. "I told you I'd bring you the stick."

Raya stepped into the corridor and shut the door behind her. "It's not big enough to do any damage."

"Oh, come on—now you're being picky."

She took the stick and whipped it through the air experimentally. "Nope." She handed it back to him as they walked down the stairs.

Phoenix tossed it to the curb outside. "How about you just forgive me for having an angel watch out for you? Most mortals would appreciate that, I would think."

"I'm not most mortals."

"True."

"But…I can let this go." Raya nudged him playfully, nearly sending him into traffic. "Where are we meeting Justine, anyway?"

"At an abandoned railroad track south of here." He flagged down a passing cab and inquired if the driver would take them to their destination. Having received an affirmative answer, Phoenix held the passenger door for Raya and hopped in after her.

The snug backseat meant closer quarters than he had imagined.

"You're going to end up sitting in my lap, little prince, if this guy takes a sharp corner." Raya gestured toward the driver as the cab sped down the street.

"Don't call me that. Especially not in front of Justinian." He realized his tactical error as soon as the words left his mouth. Telling Raya not to do something was as good as guaranteeing she would do it.

"Why am I coming, anyway? Shouldn't you supernatural beings sort this out amongst yourselves? Not that I mind—I mean, it's not every day you get to meet an angel."

"He just wants to attack me—but you, he might be curious about. I doubt he's even seen a witch while he's been in hiding. He'd probably be just as curious about you as you are about him."

"So you're banking on his curiosity outweighing his desire to hit you with a flaming sword?"

"That about sums it up."

"I feel like a human shield."

Phoenix smirked. "In a way, Witchiepoo, you are."

"Don't call me that."

"Witchiepoo."

She caught his gaze with a challenging stare. "Little prince."

The driver looked in his rearview mirror and raised his eyebrows at them.

Raya subsided. "Fine. It's more adventure than I'll get in a lifetime once I get back home. Might as well enjoy it while it lasts."

They arrived at a small park and stepped out onto the sidewalk. "Got your flashlight?"

Raya nodded and patted her bag.

"This way." Phoenix gestured toward a line of trees in the distance.

They crossed through and clambered down a hill that ended at an overgrown railroad track that hadn't been used in years. A short walk along the track led them to a rocky outcropping.

Justine stood in the shadow of the rocks. She greeted them with a nod. "Are you sure you want to do this, Phoenix?"

"He's got the sword. He's the only one who can help. So, yes. Otherwise I don't normally seek social calls with beings who are trying to injure me. Do you have a map? Where do we find him?"

Justine shook her head. "No map. He'll find you—if he wants to."

Raya made a skeptical face. "We're supposed to just wander around underground and hope he shows up? Aren't you coming?"

"I promised I would not intrude on his retreat. I am breaking the spirit, but not the letter, of that promise. I cannot say it does not trouble me."

Angels and their scruples. Phoenix swallowed a sarcastic remark. "That reminds me. Cosmo had a message for you, Justine. She said she hadn't found another bakery yet that she liked as much as yours. She also said if I didn't pass along the message, she'd break my face."

Justine chuckled. "Sounds like Cosmo."

Phoenix turned to Raya. "Shall we?"

Raya looked around. "How do we go in?"

"We go down." He led her behind the rocks to a dark opening in the ground. "Normally, you'd need ropes."

She knelt and peered into the blackness. "Normally, I'd need a tranquilizer."

"Unfortunately, all you have is me."

Raya gave him a very strange look. "You'll have to do."

Justine stepped back to give them space.

Phoenix unfurled his wings. "I'll carry you down."

Raya hesitated. "You'll drop me."

He tilted his head. "Seriously? You think I'd go to all this trouble just to drop you?"

She rose and approached him.

They stood toe-to-toe.

He wrapped his arms around her and felt the sharp intake of her breath as it quickened under his embrace. He kept his voice as steady as possible. "You'll have to hold on to me."

Raya wrapped her arms around his back, below his wings.

He indicated his chest with a nod. "Rest your head here, so there's no danger of hitting it as we descend."

She made eye contact briefly, then complied, slowly nestling her head near his shoulder.

"Ready?"

"If you drop me, I'll—"

"Hush." He raised one hand and smoothed it over her hair. "I won't."

Raya held him tighter. "Ready."

Phoenix flapped his wings, sending them both upward to hover over the cave entrance, before dropping in a controlled descent through the opening in the ground.

The sunlight disappeared in seconds as they plunged into the tunnel. They landed softly on the sandy floor.

Phoenix released his hold and wished the descent had been just a bit longer.

Raya withdrew her arms and adjusted the bag on her shoulder. "It's cold." She pulled out the flashlight and turned it on.

The light revealed chiseled limestone walls surrounding a narrow, low-ceilinged passage. Above, the entrance appeared as small as a pinhole.

Phoenix's hand brushed the stone. "Not a very cheerful place to hide out. I would have picked someplace sunny, like a deserted island."

"I thought these tunnels were filled with bones. Like an ossuary." She walked with great care, checking the ground before she placed her feet.

"Only a very small part. Most of the caves and tunnels are devoid of—shall we say—human decor."

"How far do the tunnels go?"

"Almost two hundred miles."

Raya whistled. "Wouldn't want to get lost down here."

"People do this for fun, you know. Exploring the tunnels. There are secret entrances all over Paris, which gives it an air of mystery—not to mention that it's highly illegal to wander around down here. It's irresistible to a certain type."

They turned a corner.

The sound of running water echoed through the tunnel.

She stopped. "I am not walking in whatever liquid is running through here."

"Neither am I. We'll stick to the dry tunnels." Phoenix ducked a low-hanging stone. "Mind your head."

They continued through the twisting tunnels of the old quarry until the passageway opened up to a larger, room-like space decorated with elaborate graffiti. Broad pieces of stone stacked along one of the walls formed what appeared to be a tiered seating area.

Raya sat down on the lowest tier and propped the flashlight in a crevice. "So far, no angels."

Phoenix settled on the stone next to her. "We may need to get his attention."

Raya retrieved her wand. "With magic?"

"Justine said he'd notice it."

"Should we both do something?"

Phoenix raised an eyebrow. "Don't you think all that power you're loaded up with will draw enough attention?"

She met his gaze. "Are you scared he'll notice you and get mad before he even shows up?"

"I resent that remark."

"You resemble it." She stood up. "Come on. Showtime."

"What do you want me to do?"

Raya looked him up and down. "You've been wearing that outfit ever since you got to Paris. Show me something else. Give me a dark prince fashion show—that should put off enough magic to attract attention."

"You're not serious."

"Do you have a better idea?"

Phoenix sighed and stood up. "I like this look."

"And I like fresh air and sunlight. Stop stalling and let's do this." Raya held her wand out.

The crystal at the tip began to glow.

He eyed the crystal. "What are you going to do?"

Raya smiled faintly without taking her concentration from the wand. "Have some fun."

Strands of red light snaked from the wand like electricity escaping from a novelty glass globe. The light wound around Raya and twisted behind her back, tracing a wing-shaped outline before filling in the open space with an airy filigree of crimson light.

A light sweat shone on Raya's brow. "What do you think?"

"Imitation is the sincerest form of flattery." He extended his wings as well as he could in the cramped space, mirroring her illusionary wings with his own.

"Your turn." She looked up from the crystal and let the illusion dissipate, its magic winking out in the darkness.

"What are the fashionably dressed dark princes wearing these days?" Phoenix held a finger to his jaw, as if giving the question great consideration. He snapped his fingers and altered his outfit to a particularly well-tailored example of a black three-piece suit.

"Do you even need to snap your fingers?"

"No, but it's fun."

She assessed his ensemble with a long look. "Not very practical for crawling around caves."

"You can't be satisfied, can you?"

Raya laughed. "No, I like it! It reminds me of what you were wearing the night we met—but go ahead and try something else."

He snapped his fingers again. This time, he appeared in black satin knee breeches, an elegant white shirt with lace trim, and a fine black overcoat with gold buttons.

"Oh, now you're just teasing me." Raya came up to him and took one lapel in her fingers. "You know this isn't appropriate for a quarry." She smoothed the fabric and released it.

Phoenix snapped his fingers and reverted to his usual appearance.

"There's the Phoenix I know. Ridiculous leather jacket and all."

"May I remind you, witch, that you insisted on acquiring a rather similar one for yourself?"

"Did I?" Raya looked away and fiddled with her wand. "I don't recall."

"You—"

They both froze as another light pierced the darkness of the cave.

24

A man walked into the room from a second entrance, his headlamp sweeping a blinding glare across the room.

Raya shielded her eyes.

"Bonjour." His French accent was rough as gravel, but warm as cognac. His workmanlike clothing puffed clouds of cave dust as he took a seat on a stone.

"Bonjour, friend." Phoenix positioned himself casually between the newcomer and Raya.

"Friend?" He switched off his headlamp, displaying the thick muscles of his forearms. "An Englishman in the caves, eh? And an Englishwoman?" He glanced at Raya.

"American," said Raya, who couldn't seem to take her eyes off him.

"The colonies. Of course." He nodded to himself and smoothed a thick hand over his bald head.

Phoenix compared the man before him to his memory of Justinian. Hadn't Justinian sported waves of billowing hair? Immaculate white robes? Ridiculously over-the-top gladiator sandals? The man perched on the stone showed no glimmers of magic, angelic or otherwise—but then, angels were known for their ability to go unnoticed.

However, they weren't very good at lying.

"So you're French, then?"

The man looked at Phoenix, a mild expression on his face. "French? I suppose I am."

Phoenix couldn't tell if this was an artful evasion or simply an odd sense of humor. Or both. "Were you born here?"

His chuckle sounded more like a rumble. "No."

Raya tried a question. "How long have you been exploring the caves?"

He looked at the ceiling as he considered his answer. "A long time. Maybe even a very long time."

Bored of the twenty questions game, Phoenix peered closer. Surely there would be a telltale sign.

The man noticed Phoenix's careful study. He genially patted his clothing. "Is my shirt unbuttoned, friend?"

His ironic emphasis on the last word set off warning bells.

Then he stood, unfolding like a mountain on legs, and came within arm's reach of Phoenix. "You ask a lot of questions."

Phoenix shrugged and tried to look nonchalant. "You reminded me of someone, that's all."

"Do I?" The rumble in his voice deepened.

"An old friend." He tried to edge backward without drawing attention to the fact that he was edging backward.

With one heavy step, the man closed the distance. "I don't think I'm your friend."

Raya quietly positioned her wand to point in his direction.

The man looked at her briefly before returning his gaze to Phoenix. "That won't help you, *ma chérie*."

She lowered it. "How do you—"

He removed his headlamp and held it in his hand. The light blazed, then elongated to form a column of fire. The straps twisted around themselves into a handle, which he gripped tightly as he raised the flaming sword to Phoenix's neck. The crackling edge emitted a hissing sound. "You have one chance to explain."

"It would be a lot easier if you didn't hold a sword to my neck, Justinian—ow!" Phoenix winced as the angel brought it even closer.

"I should send you to oblivion right now. Then I wouldn't have to look at your ugly face again for a very long time."

Raya stood up and slowly approached. "What did he do to you?"

"Maybe we shouldn't get into this right now—" Phoenix had to stop talking when Justinian brought the hissing blade another fraction of an inch closer.

"This *rois de cons*—"

"That's 'king of idiots,'" said Phoenix, for Raya's benefit.

"Shut up, I'm talking to the lady." Justinian repositioned the sword with its tip at Phoenix's throat.

"Oh, a lady! I like that." Raya slipped closer to Justinian and smiled.

Justinian returned the smile while keeping the sword in place. "My apologies, madame. I did not mean to frighten you. This *beauf*—"

"Uneducated rube," said Phoenix.

Justinian shot him a warning glare. "This *beauf* started a riot that tore down priceless statues at Notre Dame."

"In my defense, they were already very angry. I just suggested they hold a demonstration and demand their rights."

Raya stared at them. "When was this, exactly?"

"The French Revolution," said Phoenix.

Her eyes widened. "You started the French Revolution?"

"I didn't start it, okay? And they had a lot to be mad about, let me tell you!"

Justinian growled. "They stormed my cathedral, thinking the statues were of French kings, and then they dragged the statues to the guillotine and beheaded them."

Phoenix rolled his eyes. "Oh, I'm sorry—I was a little more concerned about people who didn't have enough bread to eat than propping up the status quo and a bunch of old statues of saints!"

"You weren't concerned about the people—you just wanted to cause trouble!"

"You just wanted to keep things as they were!"

Demon and angel glared at each other.

Raya delicately and fearlessly stepped between them, facing Justinian. "We all make mistakes," she said soothingly, patting his muscular shoulder until he slowly lowered the sword to his side.

Phoenix peeked around Raya. "By the way, what happened to your hair?"

Justinian's eyes narrowed. "You see? He is nothing but a troublemaker!"

"Yes, yes—I know." Raya spoke like someone calming a child. "Your sister said as much."

"My sister? You talked to Justine?"

"She's doing really well for herself, you know. Cutest little bakery I ever saw."

Phoenix stood in awe of Raya's skill at transitioning from dire peril to family-oriented small talk.

Justinian looked troubled. "She leaves me things, sometimes."

Raya playfully smacked his sword arm. "You should pop up for a visit. Don't you get bored down here?"

"Well—I do have a library in my cave."

"A library? Down here?"

Justinian scuffed his toe in the sand. "It's nothing, really."

"Listen, Phoenix is very sorry for what he did." Raya caught Phoenix's eye and winked.

"Oh—yes! Terribly sorry, mate."

The angel raised a skeptical eyebrow.

Phoenix smiled in what he hoped was a charming manner. "Did you know they finally found the heads?"

Justinian's face turned thunderous again.

Raya's lips pressed together as she caught Phoenix's gaze again and shook her head almost imperceptibly. "And Phoenix would like to do whatever it takes to make it up to you."

Phoenix did a double take. "I would?"

Raya nodded serenely. "Of course you would. Just like you said."

"He said that?" Justinian regarded Phoenix with surprise.

"Absolutely," said Raya.

Phoenix put on a look of humble contrition.

Raya placed a hand on Justinian's considerable bicep. "Why don't we go to your cave and talk about it?"

In one swift movement, Justinian returned the flaming sword to its earlier form and settled the headlamp in place on his forehead. "All right. But one false move, demon—" He pointed a finger at Phoenix.

"Yes, yes. I get it. Flaming swords and flying heads. No problem."

Justinian turned away, his broad back flexing as he headed deeper into the tunnels.

25

Phoenix reached out a hand to slow Raya as they followed Justinian through the twisting corridors of rough-hewn limestone. The delay gave him just enough space to whisper without fear of being overheard. "Why did you tell him that? We're here to ask him a favor, and now he's expecting me to do something for him?"

"Oh, and you were doing so well on your own? You're lucky I was there to stop him!"

The light from Justinian's headlamp swept over them both as he turned his head. "Watch your step. There is water in the next room."

They entered a high-ceiling cavern that echoed with the sound of water falling in single droplets from the stalactites above to an underground lake that stretched into the distance. The sandy path dead-ended at the water's edge.

Justinian stopped. "I will have to fly you across, mortal." He held out his hand. "Fear not." Wings the color of old parchment bloomed from his back.

Phoenix felt an illogical stab of jealousy. Damn all angels and their cursed gallantry.

Raya stepped forward and took Justinian's hand. She patted it, then released it. "Thank you. But Phoenix needs the practice."

Phoenix's jaw dropped. "I—what?"

Justinian regarded Phoenix. "He is an untrustworthy fiend. Are you sure, madame?"

Raya turned her gaze to him and her eyes glittered in the weird light of the cave. "Should I be sure, Phoenix?"

Strange feelings flashed through Phoenix as he looked into her eyes. This was about more than just carrying her across a body of water.

Justinian watched them both.

Phoenix held her gaze. "Yes. You should. I carried you once, I'll carry you again. I'll never let you fall." He swept her off her feet and into his arms so fast she squeaked.

The angel nodded once, almost as if in approval, then took off and glided across the water.

Phoenix unfolded his wings and followed, holding Raya tightly. They reached the other side. He set her down gently.

Raya placed one hand on his cheek. "Thank you." She turned to follow Justinian.

Phoenix wanted to say something—anything—but his thoughts tripped over themselves and nothing came out. He hurried to catch up as they preceded him through a gap in the stone.

A sharp turn revealed an arched opening made of weathered stone blocks.

Justinian removed the headlamp and allowed it to transform into a flaming sword, providing radiant illumination as they entered a large chamber beyond the arch. He placed the sword into a grate, from which it shed flickering firelight over the room.

Stone niches lined the walls, each filled with books stored in neat rows. A smooth-topped boulder served as a spartan table, its surface covered with more books and a few empty boxes from Justine's bakery. A wooden rack, dark with age, held an assortment of dusty bottles.

Justinian piled up the books on the table, each one releasing a puff of dust as it landed. "Forgive the mess. I have not had visitors in—"

"Forever?" Raya ran her fingers over the bookshelves.

Phoenix looked around for a place to sit and found a stone bier. He hopped up and sat with legs dangling. "It has a certain rustic charm."

Justinian gestured to a stone shaped like an ottoman. "Madame?"

"Call me Raya, please." She lowered herself to sit on the stone.

"Raya." He made a short bow in her direction.

Phoenix scowled. The showoff. He chose his next words carefully, aiming for sincerity—or at least the semblance of it. "What can I do, Justinian, to make up for my error in judgment over two hundred years ago?" Angels, the world champion grudge-holders.

The light of the sword flickered in Justinian's eyes. "How much does she know?"

"Who, Raya?" Phoenix allowed himself a small smile. "Some. Not everything. But you can speak freely."

"What do you mean, I don't know everything?"

"I should think that was obvious."

She stuck her tongue out at him.

Justinian observed the exchange. "Are you two finished with—whatever that was?"

"Quite," said Phoenix. He glared at Raya, who smiled and made a rude gesture at him out of Justinian's line of sight.

"There is something you can do for me." Justinian picked up a book, riffled the pages absently, and replaced it. "I want you to find God."

Raya leaned over so far she nearly fell off her seat. "What?"

"That's impossible." Phoenix ran his hand through his hair. "No one knows where they are."

"They?" Raya looked utterly baffled. "They who?"

Phoenix gave Justinian a shall-I-tell-her-or-shall-you look.

Justinian shrugged.

Phoenix sighed. "Our respective bosses. God. Lucifer. We don't know where they are."

Raya pointed up with one hand and down with the other. "Heaven? Hell?"

"That's the problem." Justinian gestured with one powerful hand. "We don't know where those are, either."

"Are you kidding me?" Raya's voice veered into high-pitched disbelief.

"It is not well-known among mortals," Justinian said.

Raya shook her head as if clearing it. "Wait—how do you not know where heaven and hell are?"

"Ask any angel, or demon, what they remember before coming to awareness on this mortal earth. Unless they're lying, they'll tell you they remember nothing."

Raya looked to Justinian for confirmation.

He nodded.

"Nothing? Really?" said Raya.

"Nothing," said Phoenix.

"How did you know what to do?"

"I knew my name, my rank, and my mission. Nothing more."

Raya's eyes were very round. "Like an amnesia victim."

Justinian pulled the sword from the grate and swung it through the air. "We fulfilled our duties. We fought, wrestling for the souls of mankind." He replaced the sword in its holder. "But the years weighed heavily upon us. Angels and demons alike withdrew from the battle until only a handful remained."

Phoenix smirked. "Mostly because none of us knew what the point was anymore. Humans certainly didn't need help sinning—and once they really got going, they didn't want an angel telling them to stop. Am I right, Justinian?"

"You are right, demon."

"In that sense, you were right, Raya, when you called demons a bunch of pleasure-seeking dilettantes. We are." Phoenix got up and picked up a dusty bottle from the rack. He blew the dust away and examined the label. "I partied myself into oblivion. Others, like my friend Andromalius, played at being human."

"So did Justine," said Raya.

Phoenix put the bottle back in the rack. "Exactly."

"I hid from the world." Justinian's face took on a doleful look.

"Don't be so hard on yourself, mate. We did what we had to do to stay sane. Well, sane enough, anyway."

"If you will help, and Justine, perhaps we can find our purpose again." Justinian's hopeful expression reminded Phoenix of a dog wanting to play fetch.

Phoenix had zero interest in finding a purpose, especially if it involved work, but there was a tiny part of him that felt sorry for Justinian. "I'm sure we can. You'll be basking in glory in no time. By the way, is there a reason you stopped wearing your angelic warrior getup?" Phoenix glanced around the room as if there might be a long wig, a robe, and sandals hidden in a corner.

"It did not suit me anymore. This"—he gestured to his clothing—"is not out of place among the *cataphiles*—the explorers who visit the caves. I talk to them, sometimes."

Phoenix patted him on the back. It felt like patting a tree trunk.

He looked at Phoenix with a new gleam in his eye. "Maybe I should change now, if we are going to go searching for the deity."

Phoenix and Raya exchanged alarmed glances.

Phoenix cleared his throat. "Soon. Very soon. We'll get right on that, only—" Having boxed himself into a corner, he looked to Raya.

Raya stood. "Only we need to remove a threat to Phoenix— and the rest of the demons—first."

26

Phoenix gravitated to the bottle rack and held another bottle up to the light. "Madeira," he murmured. "Hey, Justinian—can I crack one of these open?"

Justinian took the bottle from his hands. "Very old. Very delicate. You would not appreciate the nuances." He cradled it like a baby.

"I beg your pardon. I have been tasting wines practically since wine was invented. Ask Raya."

Raya rolled her eyes. "Oh, he drinks a lot, I'm sure."

Phoenix put his hands on his hips. "That is not what I meant and you know it."

Justinian carefully set the bottle on the stone table. "On the other hand, it has been a while. I have not shared a drink with anyone in a—"

"Very long time," Phoenix finished. "Well, then—no time like the present." He rubbed his hands together. "Got a corkscrew?"

"No." Justinian looked around as if one might suddenly reveal itself.

"Use the sword," said Raya.

Justinian blinked. "I suppose…"

"Brilliant." Phoenix reached for the flaming weapon, but Justinian blocked him with a powerful arm.

"I will do it." He drew the sword from the grate, then picked up the bottle, holding it at an angle, and struck the neck. The top went flying and clattered out of sight. He handed Raya the bottle. "Be careful. The opening is sharp."

Raya sniffed the contents. "Are you sure it's safe?"

"It is safe."

Raya tipped the bottle and swallowed a sip of the liquid. She coughed. "It's strong, but—wow!"

Phoenix took it. "Mortals are paying thousands of dollars per sip for something like this. Let's see how it holds up." He drank. Notes of apricot, pipe tobacco, and rose petals filled his senses, sending his thoughts to the far past when the wine might have been bottled. "Bloody hell—this is sublime." His gaze locked with Raya's, and his next thought, irrationally, was to kiss her.

She looked away, but a light blush glowed from her cheeks.

Justinian took the bottle and drank. "Ah! The good old days." He sat down. "Now tell me of your great threat." For the first time—possibly ever—his eyes twinkled with something close to mirth.

"My dear Witchiepoo, here, got mixed up with a witch who decided it would be a good idea to capture all of the demons in Paris for his personal use."

Justinian eyed Raya. "You have strange taste in friends."

"He's not my friend. We were working together in the forest of Fontainebleau. He and another witch needed a third to draw from a source of power they couldn't handle on their own."

The angel raised his eyebrows. "So? This is what witches do, is it not?"

"I didn't know quite how much power they were talking about until I was in the thick of it, and it was too late to stop."

Phoenix held his hand out for the bottle. "I went after the witch, but he overpowered me—in a dream, mind you."

Justinian handed it to him. "Why did you go after him? That was foolish, even for you." He glanced at Raya. "Were you jealous?"

Phoenix nearly spat his mouthful of vintage Madeira on the floor. "What—" he sputtered.

Justinian displayed an innocent countenance. "Just trying to understand. Go on."

Raya picked up the thread of the story. "The witch—Nathan—turned Phoenix into a cat, promising he would find him and bind him as soon as he could. And that he would come after the other demons, too. That he knew where they were."

Justinian looked at Phoenix. "You were all together?"

"We had a hangout, yes. Cosmo's bar."

"That's a name I haven't heard in—"

"A very long time," finished Phoenix.

The angel rubbed his hands over his bald head. "It is lonely for us, sometimes."

Phoenix and Raya looked at each other, then looked at Justinian again.

"This is an imbalance, Justinian. Surely you can see that. It's like"—Phoenix paused as he searched for a proper metaphor—"the branches of government. Checks and balances. Witches, angels, demons. No one gets too powerful for their own good and puts the rest of us in jeopardy."

"You want me to use the sword to take his power away?"

"You can stay here if you want to. Just lend me the sword."

Justinian laughed, a deep belly laugh that sounded like it came from the bottom of a whisky barrel. "Lend you the sword?" He slapped his knee and doubled over.

Raya covered a smile.

Great. The angel would make a fool of him in front of Raya. "I promised I'd help you find God—"

Justinian sat up and wiped tears from his eyes. "I'm sorry. I did not mean to mock you. But surely you can see—" His chest shook as he suppressed another laugh.

"You know as well as I do a witch can't just take power from another witch, but—fine." Phoenix downed another swig. "Keep your flaming sword and leave your fellow supernatural beings to rot."

Justinian's face went from angelic mirth to gathering storm clouds in an instant. "Are you questioning my honor?"

Phoenix debated whether to push his buttons or back down. It was too late to back down. "What honor?"

The angel bounded out of his seat with a roar. He seized the sword and swung it over his head before aiming it squarely at Phoenix's chest. "Never question my honor!"

Raya made as if to intervene, but Phoenix held her off with a subtle gesture. "I'm sorry. I must have misunderstood what you said."

Justinian stared at him down the length of the sword. "You did?"

"I thought you meant you wouldn't help us. You only meant that you had to come with us, didn't you?" Phoenix smiled encouragingly, only half convinced the angel would fall for it.

The sword dipped as Justinian thought this through. "Yes, of course. That is what I meant. I will come with you." He lowered the sword and looked confused.

"Wonderful!" Phoenix clapped his hands together, then pointed to an unopened bottle. "Do you mind if I take one of these to go?"

⋅•⋅

They emerged from the caverns to find Justine keeping watch on the entrance. She gasped and ran forward, throwing her arms around Justinian.

He hugged her and patted her back. "It's been a long time, sister."

She pulled back and held him at arm's length to look at him before folding him into another embrace. "Too long!"

Raya pressed her hand to her heart as she watched the angels reunite. "Apart for so long…"

Phoenix shifted uncomfortably. "But they're together now—isn't that what matters?"

"Why would anyone waste so much time?" she murmured.

Phoenix didn't blink. He just raised one eyebrow. "Why, indeed."

27

Raya adjusted her sunglasses and leaned back in the outdoor cafe chair. "I still think this is a monumentally stupid idea."

Phoenix tipped his sunglasses down and looked at her. "And yet—here you are." He slid the sunglasses back into place with a graceful push of his finger.

"We're like sitting ducks." Raya stuck out her bottom lip in a diminutive pout.

"If you have a better plan for talking to Lizzy—without Nathan—I'd like to hear it."

"She's sensitive, Phoenix. You don't think she'll see us coming from a mile away?"

"Hopefully, she's as curious as she is sensitive."

Raya made a sound of disbelief. Her gaze traveled across the sidewalk opposite the cafe to the entrance of the hotel where both Nathan and Lizzy stayed. "Hopefully, we'll get lucky and he won't come with her."

"You said yourself he's not interested in her."

"He's not. But they still work together."

They lapsed into silence, occasionally ordering more coffee in order to keep the table and its excellent view of the hotel doors.

Phoenix glanced up and smiled to himself. "Jackpot. Don't look now, but I think we have our quarry. Alone."

Raya nonchalantly turned to look. "It's her."

Lizzy, dressed to the nines in a color-coordinated summer outfit complete with hat, sunglasses, and fashionable straw bag, strolled casually away from the hotel.

Phoenix quickly piled a few bills on the table.

Raya stood up and slung her bag over her shoulder. "I wonder where she's going. Shopping, maybe?"

"Who knows." Phoenix stood and checked the street one more time, making sure Nathan wasn't in the vicinity. "Let's go."

They trailed Lizzy along the boulevard, hanging back as she stopped to peek in more than one shop window.

Lizzy hailed a cab.

"Now what?" said Raya.

"Haven't you always wanted to say 'Follow that car'?" Phoenix flagged down a cab.

Raya made a face. "No."

"Fine. I'll say it—in French. Now hurry up and get in."

Their cab followed Lizzy's down a wide, tree-lined boulevard, past a circular roundabout, and into a deeply forested area.

Raya read the sign aloud. "*Bois de Boulogne.*"

"Our Lizzy's going for a stroll in the park." Phoenix noted where Lizzy entered the park, then instructed the cab driver to take them a short distance past that point. They would double back and find her.

They stepped out of the cab and followed a footpath into the forest.

Raya shaded her eyes and looked down the path. "Chances are she already knows we're here."

"Then that will make it easy to find her, won't it?"

The path opened up at a formal garden centered around an old and graceful pagoda. Stately peacocks strolled the lawns, occasionally opening their tails in great fans of colorful plumage that glowed in the sun.

Raya spotted Lizzy first. "There she is!" She pointed across the lawn to an ornate rose garden.

Lizzy leaned down to the roses, burying her nose in the petals.

They crossed and approached her.

"Lizzy?"

"Raya! I knew you were around somewhere." Lizzy looked Phoenix up and down. "Is this your demon?"

Phoenix drew himself up. "I'm not her demon."

Lizzy's face was the picture of polite incomprehension.

Raya laid a warning hand on Phoenix's arm. "He's not mine—well, not in that sense."

If someone had hit him with a rose petal, he would have keeled over on the spot. In what sense, exactly, was he hers? "I don't think we've been introduced. Phoenix." He held out his hand.

Lizzy shook it and giggled. "Pleased to make your acquaintance."

"Anyway, Lizzy—could we talk to you for a minute? Somewhere more private?"

Lizzy pressed her hands to her cheeks. "How exciting!" She followed them off the footpath and onto the lawn, then squealed and came to a stop. "My shoes!" The high heels of her sandals sank into the turf, leaving deep divots. She tugged them off and carried them by the straps as she walked.

They withdrew to a small, secluded clearing behind the pagoda.

Lizzy sat on the lawn and drew her legs to the side, her bare feet nestled in the green grass. "What's the scoop?"

Raya examined the ground before carefully lowering herself to sit. "Has Nathan told you anything else about his 'hush-hush' plan?"

Before Lizzy could answer, the trees around the clearing bent in a sudden wind that sent leaves swirling through the air.

Phoenix turned in a slow circle, looking for the source of the disturbance.

He looked straight up and found it.

Justinian, who had apparently decided to revert to his gleaming white robes and leather gladiator sandals—but not his formerly flowing tresses—dropped out of the sky in a blinding corona of white light, brandishing his flaming sword like a maniac. The displaced air of his landing generated a localized thunderclap to accompany his bellow of "Fear not!" as his sandals hit the grass.

Lizzy dropped sideways in a faint.

"What the hell are you doing here? You were supposed to be waiting with Justine! Now look what you've done." Phoenix gestured to Lizzy, who lay sprawled on the grass.

Justinian's taut posture collapsed into a chagrined slouch, and his blazing light disappeared. "I did not mean to."

"Hollering 'Fear not!' like an idiot." Phoenix rolled his eyes in disgust. "What did you think would happen?" He looked Justinian up and down. "And what possessed you to dress up like that—and then leave out the hair?"

Justinian rubbed his head. "I like the bald look."

Raya chafed Lizzy's hands, to no avail. "She's out."

"Let me. It was my fault." Justinian set his sword aside and knelt beside Lizzy. He placed a large hand with surprising gentleness on her forehead. "Wake, *ma chérie*. You are safe."

Lizzy's eyelids fluttered. Her gaze landed on Justinian. "Raya? Who—"

"He's an angel. He's all right."

"Mostly," Phoenix muttered.

"An angel," Lizzy breathed. She reached out to him.

Justinian took her hand, then wrapped his substantial arm around her and helped her sit up. "My apologies, madame. I did not mean to frighten you."

"Oh, that's okay." Lizzy's hands fluttered like drunk birds, then landed on his arm. Her eyes widened. "My, you're very strong, aren't you?"

Phoenix made eye contact with Raya and stifled a laugh.

Raya was clearly struggling to contain a laugh as she introduced them. "Lizzy—the angel Justinian. Justinian—Lizzy the witch."

"*Enchantée*, I'm sure." Lizzy held her hand out and wiggled her fingers.

Justinian took her hand and kissed it gravely. "The pleasure is mine."

Phoenix snapped his fingers to break them out of their trance. "Are you two finished with—whatever that was?"

Justinian shot him a look that could have melted iron.

A distant peacock made a series of hooting, squawking noises.

"Why are you here, anyway?" Raya looked at Justinian with undisguised curiosity.

"I followed you. I wanted to know what was going on, so I dropped in."

Lizzy smiled. "Literally."

"Great. Now that we're all here and we all know each other—do you think it's possible we might bloody well get something done?"

The three of them stared at him like he was ruining their lovely outing in the park.

Raya shifted to face Lizzy. "Lizzy, Nathan threatened Phoenix—"

Phoenix snorted. "That's putting it mildly."

"And we think he intends to bind all of the demons in Paris. Or as many as he can find." Raya's voice became softer. "I know you think that's what witches do—bind demons to perform tasks—but this is a bridge too far."

Lizzy looked down and ran her fingers through the grass. "Didn't you bind your demon to begin with?"

Raya sighed. "I did. And I wasn't thinking of anything other than what I wanted at the time. If I had, I might have gone about it differently." She cast a sly look at Phoenix. "Now, he just hangs around of his own free will. For no apparent reason."

Lizzy frowned and a worry line appeared between her eyebrows. "Nathan isn't interested in demons doing small favors and odd jobs. He's interested in raw power."

"Didn't he get enough in the forest?"

"It wasn't enough for him."

Justinian changed position before speaking. "If your friend wants more power, why does he not replenish it like other witches do?"

"He says"—she hesitated and tucked her hair behind her ears—"he says it's 'not efficient.' That it's unreliable and not strong enough."

Phoenix watched Lizzy's face as she spoke. "So—what? Is he planning to use demons like a bunch of sentient batteries?"

"I don't know!" Her eyes went wide with distress. "He doesn't tell me everything."

Justinian patted her hand. "It's all right. It is not your fault."

"If she doesn't do anything to stop him, it is," Phoenix muttered. Thankfully, no one heard.

"We need your help," said Raya. "Or, at the very least, we need you to stand aside when the time comes."

Lizzy swiped her fingers quickly under one eye. "When the time comes for what?"

Raya looked at Phoenix before continuing. "Justinian is going to help us remove the power Nathan took from the forest. Without that, he won't be able to bind anyone, let alone an entire host of demons."

Lizzy looked around to each of them. "You won't hurt him, will you?"

Phoenix briefly pictured all the ways he would have liked to hurt Nathan, but kept his mouth shut.

Raya's glance and slight frown indicated she knew exactly what he was thinking. "Of course not. He'll just lose some power."

Lizzy exhaled. "As long as you're sure he won't be hurt."

"He said he was going to do it soon. Do you know any of his plans?" Raya smiled encouragingly. "Any little bit might help."

Justinian laid a careful hand on Lizzy's back and patted her in a soothing way.

She favored him with a brief smile before replying to Raya. "He said he was waiting for the right time. That it wasn't efficient to make multiple attempts."

"Very efficient, this Nathan." Phoenix considered. "My guess is he didn't want to make multiple attempts for fear of tipping the rest of us off. It was all in one go, or nothing."

Raya leaned back in the grass, closed her eyes, and tilted her face to the sun. "So what does that mean?"

"It means we need to lure him. Create a situation that's too tempting to pass up. Put all the demons in one place and let him come to us."

Raya opened her eyes and looked at Phoenix. "Isn't that risky?"

"Not if we have Justinian and Lizzy on our side."

Lizzy curled her small fingers around Justinian's hand. "On the side of the angels."

Raya winked cheekily at Phoenix. "And the demons."

PART III

RAYA & PHOENIX

28

Raya put on the leather jacket and tugged the collar into position. She rummaged in the open suitcase before zipping it all the way around. Only the smaller overnight bag remained open.

Tomorrow, she would fly home.

Phoenix watched the process from his seat at the hotel room table. "All packed?"

Raya set the suitcase upright. "All packed. Just a few things left out for tonight and tomorrow."

Phoenix stood and smoothed his hands over the shoulders of her jacket. "And this? Is this your armor for tonight?"

Raya met his gaze. "I like my armor."

"Your armor is impenetrable."

"Just like yours." She flipped one lapel of his leather jacket up in a teasing manner and let it fall back into place.

"We're not talking about jackets anymore, are we?"

"Such a clever little dark prince." She turned away and set about fixing her wand into her hair.

"Don't call me—"

"Why should I stop when I know you're enjoying yourself?" Raya smirked.

"Two can play at that game, Witchiepoo."

She laughed. "Who said I enjoyed being called that?"

Phoenix delivered his response with quiet precision. "You didn't have to."

Her mouth opened and shut. "We'd better go. We don't want to be late."

<hr>

Cosmo's bar echoed with their footsteps as they crossed the empty room. The candles in the wall sconces cast flickering shadows like ghosts across the floor.

Raya looked around. "Anybody home?"

Cosmo popped up from behind the bar. "About time you two showed up."

"You think everyone got the message?" Phoenix slid onto a stool.

"We're ready to rock." Cosmo flipped a bottle, then pointed it at Raya. "How are you going to keep the wicked witch from seeing the good witch?"

Phoenix reached over the bar and grabbed a cherry. "Courtesy of our angel-in-residence." He bit into the unnaturally red fruit.

Justine and Justinian rocketed through the window as if it weren't there. Justinian landed and folded away his parchment-colored wings. Justine skidded to a stop, brushed nonexistent dust from her shoulder, and folded away her brilliantly white wings. "My ears are burning," she said.

"Justine!" Cosmo vaulted over the bar like a gymnast and ran to Justine, throwing her arms around the angel.

"Oof! Help, I'm being attacked!" Justine threw her head back and laughed, clasping her arms around Cosmo. They staggered across the room still holding each other and collapsed into a corner booth, laughing and talking with animated gestures.

Phoenix swallowed the cherry. "Make that two angels-in-residence."

Justinian eased himself onto a stool next to Raya. "She said if I was going, she was going."

"It's not a party until the angels show up." Phoenix turned to Raya. "You ready?"

Raya nodded, hoping her nervousness didn't show on her face.

Justinian leaned back and surveyed the room. "What about Lizzy?"

"She's coming with Nathan," Raya said.

A worried look crossed Justinian's face.

Raya patted his arm. "Don't worry. Lizzy can handle herself. She's more powerful than she looks."

"She's not the only one." Phoenix stood up. "Time to go incognito, Raya." He cupped his hands around his mouth. "Justine! Stop fooling around and get your wings over here."

Justine reluctantly stood and joined them at the bar.

Cosmo followed.

The angels and the demons looked at Raya expectantly.

Raya tried to swallow but found her mouth completely dry. She cleared her throat instead. "Witches and demons can sense each other, but neither can sense angels who don't want to be noticed. We're assuming Nathan will sense a big crowd of demons—but what we don't want is for him to realize I'm here, too. That means I need to get out of sight before all the demons get here." She gestured for Justine and Justinian to follow her to an empty space away from the bar and seating area. "I need you to hide me."

Justine cocked her head and looked Raya up and down. "Let's try this. Justinian, can you extend your aura?"

Justinian's outline blazed into brightness and spread outward.

"Farther," said Justine.

The light expanded to cover Raya, who shielded her eyes.

Justine went on the other side of Raya, opposite Justinian, and lit up like a flare. The two auras intersected and overlapped with Raya on the inside.

"How's that?" said Raya. "Phoenix? Cosmo? Can you sense my presence? As a witch, I mean?"

Phoenix squinted into the glare. "Nothing."

"You're good," said Cosmo.

"Now we wait," said Justinian.

Their voices sounded like they'd been muffled with blankets. Raya covered her eyes completely from the dazzling glow. "This is awkward."

Phoenix chuckled. "Look at it this way—it's nowhere near as awkward as calling in a legion of demons to bait the trap, then having Nathan high-tail it because he sensed your presence."

Someone brought Raya a chair, although she couldn't see who, thanks to the blinding light between Justine and Justinian. She knew more demons would be arriving any minute but couldn't tell which ones or how many since the shielding light seemed to work both ways. It made the suspense of waiting much worse.

The familiar voices retreated until she could no longer hear them at all. Raya shifted in the chair. She hadn't felt this alone since the plane touched down at the airport. She inhaled and exhaled, keeping her breath even as it went in and out.

Phoenix would be there, even if she couldn't see him now—and Cosmo, and Justine, and Justinian, and even George with his funny coat and antique glasses.

And Lizzy, too—Lizzy would be on their side.

Raya sincerely hoped Lizzy would be on their side. Her stomach flipped at the momentary doubt.

This would not go down in flames, not if she had anything to say about it. A grim smile touched her lips. She strained her senses, but could hear nothing but a distant buzz of conversation. The minutes ticked by, leaving her to fidget restlessly.

Suddenly, the murmur of the crowd collapsed into silence.

The angelic shield dropped all at once like a heavy stage curtain slashed free of its rings.

Raya rose from the chair and drew her wand, blinking as her vision cleared of stars.

Nathan stood in the center of the room with a self-satisfied smirk on his face and Lizzy by his side. A net of green light radiated from his wand, billowing up and over the assembled demons before descending along the perimeter of the room. "Raya. You're just in time to join us."

Trapped within the net, the demons at the bar and tables remained in a silent tableau where only their eyes moved.

Nathan didn't appear to notice the angels—they kept themselves hidden, flanking her, awaiting her signal.

"I'm not here to join you, Nathan." She aimed her wand at the center of the magical net.

"There's enough for all of us. I'm willing to share." He glanced at Phoenix, frozen in the magic. "You can have this one—although God only knows why you'd want him."

"Go to Hell, Nathan." She silently probed for weaknesses in the net. When would Lizzy make her move?

"Your loss." Nathan shrugged. "Lizzy, lock it in. We're wasting time."

A look of annoyance passed over Lizzy's face and was swiftly hidden by a look of adoration so over-the-top it approached parody. "Of course, Nathan." She placed her hand tenderly on Nathan's cheek, then slid it to wrap around the back of his neck.

He shifted his weight uncomfortably. "What are you doing?"

A sad smile lifted her lips. She kissed his cheek. "What I should have done all along."

He gasped in shock—and not just from her words.

Raya felt Lizzy lock into Nathan's power the same way a fisherman sets a hook in a fish.

Nathan dropped to his knees at the impact. "Please—Lizzy—don't—"

"You were wrong to think I would follow you blindly." Lizzy backed away from him and slipped her hand into Raya's.

Raya squeezed her hand in solidarity as the magic linked them together. Lizzy's maneuver made it easier for Raya to seize Nathan's power as it sizzled through the air like superheated vapor. He'd extended himself severely in his attempt to bind all the demons at once. "Justinian!"

Justinian brandished the flaming sword and allowed himself to be seen.

Nathan registered the angel's presence with wild-eyed confusion. "What—"

But he had no time to complete the thought as Raya grasped the magic and hauled it in. The power barrelled toward her. She ignored the instinct to duck the impact—instead, she twisted the crashing wave into a concentrated stream and directed it to Justinian, whose sword crackled and spat fire as it drank the magic.

Raya trembled as wave after wave washed through her. She looked into Nathan's eyes as they filled with tears of rage and helplessness.

She knew what he was thinking.

She could drain it all, if she wanted to. She could leave him powerless and alone, bereft of the one thing that gave his life meaning.

She could even take the magic for herself, if she desired. Enough power to end the nightmares forever.

But would it?

A woman's silvery laugh echoed through her mind as images from the six medieval tapestries whirled through her vision, ending on the cryptic phrase *À Mon Seul Désir*.

To My Sole Desire.

All the power she ever wanted lay within her grasp—and yet her thoughts left the magic behind and turned to a certain dark prince in the crowd.

A spell is a flap of a butterfly wing in the right place, at the right time…

And so is love.

All the bickering, the fighting, the teasing and insults—they'd used anything to keep their feelings at bay, to prop up the walls between them, to refuse to acknowledge that not only did they truly, affectionately, passionately like each other—they *needed* each other.

Her gaze met his—and the rest of the world fell away when she saw her feelings reflected in his eyes. She was his witch, and he was her demon, and God help anyone who came between them.

Nathan collapsed to his hands and knees, keening in wordless anguish as the last remnants of the forest power tore away and landed safely within Justinian's sword. Another second and Nathan's original power would be obliterated.

Raya slammed the connection shut. Her vision darkened and the room spun.

Strong arms caught her as her knees buckled.

Phoenix caught her as she fell, wrapping his wings around her to buffer her from harm. He eased her into a comfortable position on the floor and pillowed her head with his wing as he knelt beside her.

Her eyelids fluttered and the corners of her lips lifted in a triumphant smile. "We did it."

Phoenix smoothed her hair from her forehead. "Hush, now. You've overexerted yourself."

"Have not," she murmured.

"But you must be all right—you're still arguing with me."

"Mm." Raya chuckled softly but didn't dispute the point. "Is Lizzy okay?"

"She's fine. Justinian caught her. Justine would have caught you, but I beat her to the punch."

A commotion caused both of them to look to the source of the noise.

Cosmo and Justine dragged an unresisting Nathan out the door, and—from the sound of it—none too gently down the stairs.

"And stay out!" said Cosmo, her voice floating up the stairs and into the bar.

The outer door slammed with satisfying finality.

Cosmo sauntered into the room like she owned the place—which, technically, she did—then vaulted over the bar. "Drinks on the house!"

The demons roared in approval.

Justinian and Lizzy joined George at a table, and all three of them leaned in over some ancient-looking tome George had produced from a hidden pocket.

Justine slid onto the stool nearest the absinthe fountain and began setting up glasses, slotted spoons, and sugar cubes.

Raya nestled closer to Phoenix and caressed his wing feathers. "I'm glad you caught me."

"Are you really?"

Her eyes flashed. "Don't make me tell you twice, demon."

"In that case"—he helped her sit up—"I'm going to kiss the hell out of you, witch."

"Not if I kiss you first." She threw both arms around his neck and pressed her lips to his, the impact nearly knocking him over.

He recovered and plunged his hands into the tangle of her hair, cradling her head to brace her as he returned the kiss with equal fire.

Now that was the kind of argument he could live with.

EPILOGUE

Waves crashed on the beach as low tide dragged the water farther away from Raya's lounge chair. She dug her toes into the soft, powdery sand and let the onshore breeze push her hair back.

It was good to be home.

"More sunscreen?" Phoenix held the bottle out from an adjacent lounge chair. "Wouldn't want you to burn."

Erin leaned over. "Raya's in no danger of that. You put enough sunscreen on her to float the Titanic. Pass it over."

Phoenix handed the bottle to Erin.

Erin took it and popped the cap.

From the lounge chair next to Erin, Andromalius sat up and snatched the bottle playfully. "That's my job."

Raya and Erin shared a smile as Andy smoothed the lotion over Erin's shoulders.

"So—back to school." Andy looked across to the other demon.

"Whatever shall we do, Phoenix, while the ladies continue their gainful employment?"

Raya raised an eyebrow. "You mean besides the cooking and cleaning? We already know lawn work is a wash."

"I tried to mow the lawn." Phoenix pressed a hand to his chest in a play for sincerity. "Honestly. I don't know why the lawn mower blew up."

Raya scoffed. "Probably because you got Justinian to stick a sword in it for you."

"I never!"

Raya grabbed him and pulled him closer. "Look me in the eye and lie, kitty cat—see what it gets you."

"Oh, all right." Phoenix disarmed her, as he often did, with a smile and a stolen kiss. "Her Royal Witchiness is right. I had an angel put the hellish torture device out of its misery."

Andy chuckled as he applied more sunscreen to Erin's back. "Out of your misery, more like." He capped the bottle and stuck it in the sand. "I'm sure we can find ways to stay busy. Justinian isn't going to wait forever for you to fulfill your promise."

Phoenix groaned. "Must I?"

Raya fixed him with a look. "Why else do you think he's been hanging around so much? It's not just because he loves board game night—or destroying lawn mowers."

"I'll get right on it." Phoenix leaned back and laced his fingers behind his head. "Soon."

Erin took two water bottles from the cooler. "Have you heard from Lizzy?"

"She's eager to come visit. And eager for us to come see her." Raya took the bottle Erin offered. "She's just eager, in general.

That's Lizzy." She shrugged philosophically, opened the bottle, and took a drink of cold water.

Andy reached across the gap between him and Erin to take Erin's hand affectionately. "Cosmo and Justine still in Paris?"

Raya nodded. "As far as we know."

"So's George," added Phoenix. "God knows where that arrogant witch ended up. Dead, hopefully."

"Bit harsh," said Erin.

Phoenix barked a laugh. "Oh, what, like you've never had a death wish for someone? A certain rotter named Mark, perhaps?"

Erin's lips curved in a quiet, satisfied smile. "Being Mark is its own punishment."

"Hear, hear!" said Andy. "And the kitchen renovation is going to look great." He winked.

Raya stared at the mesmerizing waves, watching the power of the water as it churned across the sand. "You should go to the next convention, Erin."

"Me?"

Phoenix buried his face in his hands. "Not another witch. I can't take more than one at a time. Please, Erin—ignore everything she says."

"Shut up, demon." Raya turned slightly to face Erin. "I mean it. I think you could benefit."

Erin's brow wrinkled in thought. "What if Nathan were there?"

Andy gasped. "He wouldn't dare."

Raya tilted her head back and forth as she considered how to respond honestly without scaring Erin off. "He might. But he'd be a fool to start something." She settled back.

The foursome looked out to sea without speaking.

Phoenix broke the silence first. "If you were God, where would you hang out?"

Raya glanced at Erin and Andy, then took Phoenix's hand, letting its warmth radiate into her fingers. She smiled. "Right here."

If you believe age is just a number and mid-life is the perfect time for magic, you'll love Kate Moseman's newest book, Silver Spells!

About the Author

Kate Moseman is a writer, photographer, and recipe developer who lives in Florida with her family.

9 781734 514438